Spring of the Poacher's Moon

Angela Dorsey

Spring of the Poacher's Moon

WHINNIES ON THE WIND –
SPRING OF THE POACHER'S MOON
Copyright: Text © 2010 by Angela Dorsey
www.angeladorsey.com
The author asserts her moral right to be identified as the author of
the work in relation to all such rights as are granted by the author to
the publisher under the terms and conditions of this agreement.
Original title: As above
Cover and inside illustrations: © Jennifer Bell 2010
Cover layout: © Stabenfeldt A/S

Typeset by Roberta L. Melzl
Editor: Bobbie Chase
Printed in Germany, 2010

ISBN: 978-1-934983-55-3

Stabenfeldt, Inc.
225 Park Avenue South
New York, NY 10003
www.pony.us

Available exclusively through PONY.

Blood, fire,
Greed-sick ones
Roaring near us,
Searching

Vile, menace,
death sticks pointing
Eager to harm,
Hunting

Flee, hide,
Innocence running
Never linger,
Escape!

The world must've ended. Mom was actually riding into town. I kept shaking my head, even as I rode my best horse friend, my gorgeous gray gelding, Rusty, beside her. This all had to be a bizarre dream. Mom – *my mom* – going to town? Unbelievable!

You think I'm overreacting? Then you don't know my mom. She's a hermit; a recluse, a woman who moved out into the bush with her baby – me – almost thirteen years ago and hasn't left since. Not once. Zilch. Nada!

I first knew it would be a momentous day when that morning she casually announced that she wanted to ride over to Kestrel's family's ranch, five miles away, to use their radiophone. It's been two years since she's even done that.

Anyway, we rode for an hour to reach Kestrel's house, and when we arrived they gave Mom the unwelcome news that their radiophone wasn't working – something about a dead battery – and lo and behold, Mom said it was *imperative* that she make a certain call and that we would continue into town. I was so surprised I almost fell out of Rusty's saddle.

Because of Mom, I don't get out much. In fact, I haven't been to town for five years. The last, actually *only,* time I went was with Kestrel and her family. Unfortunately, after I got out of her sight, Mom had major second thoughts about me being in civilization – as if one general store and twenty houses can be called civilization – and she never let me go again. Still, I treasure that one precious escapade to our miniscule town. To see more than one house in one place? Wow! And there was *traffic!* I even went into a real store and bought a candy bar. It was the coolest thing. And just in case you think I'm too weird for finding something so mundane to be so awesome, imagine never having gone into a store before in your *entire life*!

Yes, that's me; Evy, the wild girl.

Luckily, I'm not as mentally unstable as you might think, because I read a lot. But it's one thing to experience something in a book and quite another to do it in real life. And besides, I've never read about someone buying a candy bar in a store. Apparently, it's too boring to write about – but trust me, if you've never even *seen* a store before, buying a candy bar is quite exhilarating. Just thinking about it makes me giddy.

But enough rambling. As I was saying, I was riding

beside my mom and we were going to town. Kestrel, my best friend, rode with us so she could show us where the one payphone was.

And the purpose for this *imperative* phone call? I deduced it had something to do with Edward, my mom's agent, who sells her paintings in his fancy Vancouver gallery. In the spring and fall, he takes her share of the money from the sale of her paintings and buys our supplies with them, then brings them to our remote cabin and picks up more paintings to sell. I guessed that for some unknown mysterious reason, Mom wanted to add something to the supply list she'd mailed him, and that this something was important enough to actually ride into town for – for the first time in almost thirteen years! So *now* can you understand why I was so blown away?

I could tell Mom was a bit overwhelmed too. I know her better than anyone. Her face was pale and her breathing shallow, and with every step closer to civilization she became more obviously distressed. Kestrel and I were chatting about Twilight, my yearling filly, when Kestrel pointed to my mom's back and mouthed, *What's wrong with her?*

I shrugged. Like I could tell her anything with Mom right there. Besides, Kestrel knew about Mom's hermit tendencies. Maybe she just didn't know how strong they were.

"How long until we get there?" I asked in my best whiny voice, trying to lighten Mom's mood.

She looked back at me with a scowl, then realized I was joking and scowled harder.

"I need to go to the bathroom," Kestrel complained, getting into the spirit of things.

"Mo-om, I'm hungry."

"Me too."

"Mo-om."

"That's enough," said Mom. Her voice was tight. Okay, so she didn't find us very funny...

I raised my eyebrows at Kestrel to prepare her for my future mischievousness. "So who are you phoning anyway?" I asked Mom for about the tenth time that day. She hadn't answered the other times, but this time I was asking in front of Kestrel. Mom might be too embarrassed to say nothing.

She didn't even turn her head. So much for social pressure.

"Twilight!" Kestrel called beside me.

I turned in the saddle. Twilight sniffed at an ordinary patch of dirt, far behind us, apparently mesmerized.

Twilight, keep with us, I thought to her and she raised her head. Her black rimmed eyes, ears, and nostrils set off the burnished gold of her body perfectly. How lucky I was to have such a wonderful filly.

No. She turned her back to me, then began to nibble some grass.

Okay, so make that lucky to have such a wonderful, if irritatingly independent, filly.

I huffed at her, then decided she was getting too much satisfaction from my irritation and decided to ignore her. I know from experience that it's no fun being sassy if no one cares what you do.

It worked. She wanted me to be upset with her, and when I wasn't she felt bored. She sprang into a gallop and raced up behind us.

"Wow, she's coming because I called her," said Kestrel. "I don't believe it."

"She's getting better at listening, I think," I answered, still privately feeling irritated but refusing to say so. I couldn't tell Kestrel that the only reason the filly ran after us was because I was ignoring her.

No one knows my secret, you see. It's not that I'd mind sharing. I'm just afraid Kestrel will think I'm a freak and not want to hang out with me anymore. And besides, how do you bring up something like that? 'Hey Kestrel, I'm a psycho nutcase who can telepathically talk to horses...'? Yeah, right.

One of my biggest mistakes was thinking I could tell my mom. Even though that was years ago, she still questions me sometimes, searching for personality glitches. I think she's afraid she's damaged my delicate psychological balance by making me grow up in the bush. But the talking to horses thing has nothing to do with that. It's just a gift I have. Or a curse. I haven't figured out which yet. It's certainly gotten me into trouble at times, that's for sure.

Twilight drew alongside Rusty, slowed to nip him playfully on his iron gray shoulder, and then surged forward. Snorting, she swept past Cocoa, Mom's chocolate brown mare, and disappeared around a corner in the rough road ahead of us.

Twilight! Come back! I mind-shouted after her.

Amusement swirled back to me. She thought I was being funny, trying to order her around.

"Evy, you need to get a rope on her," said Mom. "We'll be coming across more ranches soon, and maybe even a vehicle."

"Yeah, okay." Mom was right. Twilight had no idea what civilization was like. Not that I was an expert or anything.

Twilight. Danger. Come back.

"Twilight!" Kestrel called beside me.

I felt the filly slow and then turn. One thing she'd learned as a wild horse – trust your herd mates when they say there's danger. She met us on the corner and I slid off Rusty's back with the lead rope in my hand. Twilight let me clip the rope to her halter without a quibble. First, she's Miss Wild-and-Free and now she's all domestic. Was I ever going to figure her out?

"I should be a horse trainer," said Kestrel. "That's the second time Twilight's listened to me."

I climbed back into Rusty's saddle, Twilight's lead rope in my hand. "You should be. Maybe we can be world famous horse trainers together."

Kestrel nudged her mare, Twitchy, with her heels.

Twitchy didn't move. She's old and permanently tired. When Mom asked Cocoa to walk on, the other horses, including Twitchy, stepped out behind her. Kestrel made a face at Twitchy's flopping ears.

Where danger? Twilight asked.

Coming soon. Many humans.

Humans. Loathing and fear saturated her thoughts. I knew she considered Kestrel, my mom, and me exceptions to the rule, but still, she could've been a touch more subtle.

Stay beside Rusty and you will be safe.

Kestrel was staring at me.

"What?" I asked.

"Sometimes it's like you're completely deaf, Evy. I swear."

The hazards of carrying on two conversations at once. "Sorry."

Mom looked back at me and rolled her eyes.

"What did you say?" I asked Kestrel.

"I said, Twilight can be our number one exhibit. If an ex-wild horse comes when we call, lots of people will want us to train their horses."

"As long as she comes. You know Twilight."

"If she doesn't come, I'll just say that's a result of *your* training methods," Kestrel joked.

"Thanks." I stuck my tongue out at her.

"Listen." Mom stopped Cocoa and our horses halted behind her.

13

Twilight's head shot up, as if she'd heard a monster. I strained to hear something, and there it was – a distant rumbling.

Bear! Twilight tried to run, but the end of her lead rope was wrapped snug around my saddle horn. When she couldn't escape, fear spiked through her heart – and into mine, making me clutch Rusty's mane to stop myself from falling.

Firmly, I forced her fear through the back door of my mind.

Not bear. Truck. Safe… if you stay by me.

Yeah, you guessed it. I *feel* horse emotions too. In fact, I started out with just the feeling and moved on to developing a language with Rusty, and then recently, Twilight. Most of the time, feeling horse emotions isn't too bad. Except for the powerful emotions. They can really get me if I'm not prepared. However, because of some of the horrible experiences Twilight has had, that I felt right along with her – lucky me – I've learned how to control them.

"She's never heard a vehicle before," I said and moved Rusty to the side of the rutted, muddy road. Mom and Kestrel followed, keeping their horses between Twilight and the road.

The truck lurched around the corner, then swayed, bucked, and rattled over the ruts toward us. The driver gave us a wave as she pitched past, her eyes hidden beneath her cowboy hat. Brown pigtails flopped on her

back. Within a minute, she and her truck were out of sight, around a corner in the narrow, winding road.

"Poor Twilight," said Kestrel. "That was scary, wasn't it?"

I leaned down to pat the filly on her neck. "Do you know the driver?" I asked Kestrel absently. My mind was elsewhere; on my mom, to be exact. The moment the truck had pitched into view, she'd turned her face away from the driver and kept it away until the truck was out of sight. I know she's shy of people, but still, her reaction seemed excessive. It was almost as if she was afraid the driver would recognize her.

"Yeah, that's Caroline," said Kestrel. "She lives a few miles north of our place. She's kind of weird, but fun too. She has a kid our age. Jon. He's okay."

"He's okay? Really? I thought everyone out here was at least a little crazy."

Kestrel laughed.

Mom and Cocoa moved ahead, resolutely ignoring our conversation.

"Do you know her, Mom?"

"No."

"Maybe we should go over to her place and introduce ourselves. You need friends too." Which was true, by the way, but had nothing to do with why I was suggesting it. I wanted to weasel just a tiny bit more information from her about the biggest mystery of my life: *why* Mom didn't like people; *why* she was in hiding, because that's what it seemed like she was doing; and *who* she was

16

hiding from. A few months ago, she'd slipped up and told me we'd only be in the bush for a few more years, which made it even more of a mystery. Basically, I was trying to see if she'd slip up again. It sounds mean, I know. But I was sure that the reason she was hiding away had something to do with me, and I figured I had a right to know the reason.

"I have you, and Kestrel and her family. I don't need any more friends." This said in her creepy voice, the one that was so calm and controlled that it could have come from a robot. She wasn't going to slip up and give me more information right now.

The rest of the ride into town was uneventful, if you don't count Twilight's panic attacks. We passed two more vehicles, three horseback riders with an ultra-loud dog, and a herd of free ranging cattle before reaching the outskirts of town. Then things got really tense. Dogs rushed out from unfenced yards to sniff or growl or bark at us. Cars, trucks, and even a tractor raced past. People walked along the roads and greeted us. The people freaked Mom out even more than Twilight. Of course, I thought it was great. I mean – wow – there really are other people in the world!

All too soon, we reached the general store. Kestrel pointed out the payphone hanging next to the front door, and Mom led us around the side of the store. She dismounted Cocoa, pushed the mare's reins into my hand, and commanded us to stay put, to not wander, to not talk to anyone, to not peek around the corner to the front of the store, and so forth and so on.

The second she was out of sight, I turned to Kestrel. "I'm going to try listening to what she says."

"Me too."

I slid from Rusty's back, and immediately felt his disapproval. He had no idea what Mom had said, but he could feel me being sneaky. Horses are very truthful creatures and are nervous of deception of any kind. But how else was I going to know what was going on? "We can tie the horses to Rusty's saddle. He won't go anywhere."

Moments later, the three horses were secured, Twilight to Rusty's saddlehorn, and Twitchy and Cocoa to the leathers dangling from each side of the back of the saddle.

Stay here, Rusty. Be right back.

He laid his ears back and gave a vigorous shake of his head in protest, but I knew he'd stay.

Kestrel and I hurried to the corner of the store and slowly leaned around the edge. Mom was on the other side of the doorway, her back to us, speaking incomprehensibly into the phone. We had to get closer to hear. I motioned to Kestrel that I was going to sneak up behind her. Kestrel shook her head and motioned to the far corner. She was right. We'd probably hear her better if we were listening from the other side.

But then Mom's voice got louder.

"Oh no," she said.

I put my fingers to my lips.

"How much did I make, Edward?"

"How are we going to live on ..." She paused, as if she knew she was loud enough to overhear. "Mumble, mumble... need to eat. Evy needs... mumble... and new clothes."

Silence again as she listened to Edward say something. I felt a moment of hollow gratification. Gratification, because I was right. She had phoned Edward, and she had tried to add something to the list. Hollow, because it sounded like her paintings hadn't sold well last winter. She hadn't earned enough to add anything extra to her list, let alone pay for all the basic supplies we needed, like food and clothes.

I stepped softly around the corner. If I could just get closer, I'd be able to hear better – and I *had* to hear more.

"Actually, I'm doing something different," she said. "That might help."

Pause.

"Yes, I'm still doing landscapes. But now I'm doing horses too."

I moved one step nearer.

"You heard me right. Horses. Wild horses, to be exact." From her defensive tone, I guessed Edward didn't like that she was painting the mustangs.

"Don't judge them until you see them. And what I feel inspired to create is *not* your business."

And then she started to turn toward me.

I ran backward, my heart thumping like mad, as Mom pivoted in slow motion. I passed the corner of the store and dove to the side, just before she could see me.

My landing wasn't nearly as hard as I expected. Kind of lumpy and boney though.

"Mmmfff," said Kestrel, beneath me.

"Evy!" Mom's voice.

I scrambled off my best friend. "Yeah, Mom?" I yelled, trying to sound farther away.

A pause. An eternal, agonizing second passed. Two seconds. Three… "Nothing." Then her murmuring continued into the phone.

"Sorry," I whispered to Kestrel.

"That's okay," she said, sitting up. She rubbed her knee, then swiped at the mud clinging to her jacket. "I'm used to it. It's all part of being your best friend." Kestrel thinks I'm some kind of trouble magnet or something. I don't know why.

I hurried back to the corner and slowly leaned around the wooden edge. Mom was hunched over the phone, her hand blocking her mouth, and facing me! She said something, then saw me and pulled the receiver away from her mouth.

I was totally caught.

But she *had* called me, just moments ago… Right? "Yeah? What do you want?" I asked, trying to sound as if I hadn't been eavesdropping on her and Edward.

"What?"

"You just called me."

"Go wait for me by the horses. I'll just be one more minute."

I pulled quickly back, motioned to Kestrel to follow, and ran toward the back of the building. If we only had a minute, we'd better hurry.

Sorry. Be right back, I said to Rusty as we raced past. He looked at me, pinned his ears again and stamped his hoof. Twitchy had been trying to pull him toward a big clump of grass for the last few minutes, and I felt both his disappointment in me and his irritation at the hungry old mare.

We ran along the back of the store, dodged a rusty tractor, turned the corner – and came to a screeching halt. Two men looked at us from where they leaned against a beat up brown truck, talking: an old guy with a black cowboy hat and a young guy with a big grin.

Kestrel raised her hand in a tentative greeting. "Hi, Charlie. Hi, Troy."

"Hey, Kes. Your dad in town?" the younger man asked, obviously unaware that Kestrel prefers people to use her full first name. She likes that her name is the same as a type of small hawk.

"No, I'm here with…" Kestrel's face washed red. She knew my mom wouldn't want us saying her name, "… um, some friends."

"Looks to me like you two are planning on getting

into trouble." This suspicious comment from the old guy. He didn't sound like he was joking either. In fact, he glared at us as if he could see a myriad of secrets and schemes lurking in our eyes.

I stared back, then grabbed Kestrel's arm. "Let's get out of here." I pulled her back around the corner, then whispered in her ear, "We can't listen while they're watching anyway. We'd better get back."

Mom wasn't by the horses when we returned, thank goodness. We untied the three from Rusty's saddle and remounted, then arranged innocent looks on our faces. Rusty snorted in disgust.

And still we waited. What was taking her so long? Maybe we should have gone past the all-seeing, all-knowing old guy.

Sorry, I said to Rusty. *Trying to find out secrets.*

Should keep no secrets.

Agree. But she will not answer questions.

Rusty snorted crossly, but I could feel his mood lighten. He'd forgiven me, just a little. *Lots of oats tonight,* I promised, and I felt him brighten further.

Boots sounded on the boardwalk in front of the store. "She's coming," whispered Kestrel.

But Mom wasn't the one who came around the corner. It was the old guy. Charlie. His eyes swept over us, over our horses, and stopped on Twilight. A cold wind swirled around me – and then Mom squeezed past him. She kept her head down so he couldn't see her face and hurried toward us.

"Let's go," she said. "No questions." She swung aboard Cocoa and we turned our horses toward home. We rode past Charlie without looking at him, then Mom asked Cocoa to trot. The other horses quickened their pace as well, and we moved swiftly away from the store.

My neck prickled. Maybe it was my imagination, but I could *feel* Charlie watching us as we trotted away. I couldn't help myself; I had to look back just as we were about to round the corner. Sure enough, there he stood on the store porch, staring after us, his face hard lined and his mouth looking as if it was etched in marble. Another shiver spiraled down my spine. There was something about the way he watched us, so intent, so predator-like, that made me want to run and hide.

I told myself to stop being silly and making mountains out of molehills. I'd end up as weird about people as Mom was if I wasn't careful. Kestrel and I hadn't done anything wrong. We'd just run around a corner. We hadn't gotten into trouble and we hadn't been trying to eavesdrop on him and his friend.

Still, the prickles on my neck didn't stop until we were around the corner and Charlie was out of sight. I felt Twilight relax then too. I'd been feeling so tense that I'd hardly noticed that she'd been leery of Charlie as well.

Watching me, she said, and snorted.

I saw.

Glad he is gone.

I agreed wholeheartedly, and Rusty chimed in too – somewhat reluctantly, as he was still a touch upset with me. But apparently, the vote was unanimous. We all were nervous of Charlie and would be glad to never see him again. What nerve he had, staring after us like that! He was too rude.

After promising Kestrel that I'd ride to meet her when she came over in two days for our weekly visit, Mom and I left her parents' ranch and continued toward home. It was early evening by the time we turned off the dirt road and onto the narrow track that led to our cabin. I drooped in my saddle as we rode. I could tell Mom was worn out too by the way she rode beside me, but there was more than tiredness getting her down. Her forehead creased with worry lines and her eyes looked pained. When the look didn't disappear as we neared home, our safe place, I became even more troubled.

"Mom, is everything okay?"

She sighed.

"What did Edward say?"

"How do you know I phoned Edward?"

Uh oh. "Um, I guessed. What did he say?"

She blinked rapidly for a second or two, almost as if she was blinking back tears. Now *that* was worrisome.

I could try demanding answers, but it had never worked before. I'd tried being non-emotional and businesslike in the past too, with the same result. So maybe I'd have better luck being sympathetic and understanding.

"It must have been awful, whatever it was."

"Everything's okay, Evy."

"Is there something I can do to make things better?" I felt like such an ungrateful daughter. Why had I never asked that question before? I sucked.

Mom just shook her head and stared down at Cocoa's dark mane.

"I'd be glad to help, if there's anything I can do."

She smiled at me, but her sad eyes didn't meet mine. "There's nothing you can do. I... I... well, honestly, I just feel like such a failure sometimes."

What? Had I heard her right? My mom, the brilliant artist, the awesome mom, the wilderness survivor, the most patient home school teacher I'm sure this world has ever known, felt like a failure?

"You are so *not* a failure," I said with as much emphasis as I could muster. "Not even a little bit. Don't even *think* it."

She looked up at me, openly surprised at my vehemence.

"You're awesome," I continued. "Even though I'm not supposed to say that, being your kid and all, and after today, I'll deny I said anything. But you are. Totally great. I mean it."

Tears studded her eyes. "Really?"

I nodded. "You're my hero," I said in an oddly croaky voice. And I wasn't joking or lying or anything. My mom *is* my hero, even if she's incredibly frustrating. Even if I constantly wish she'd trust me more and tell me things.

She turned her head to stare out over Cocoa's ears. Ahead of us, Twilight glowed in the evening light as she high-stepped in a circle, her tail in the air. She sprung straight up, as if on springs, and landed on four stiff legs, then kicked up her hind end and raced around the corner. She'd be the first one home tonight.

Mom laughed. "That horse of yours is a strange one, Evy."

I was relieved to hear her laugh. Maybe, she was okay again. No one is tougher than my mom. No wonder I admire her.

"I know," she said, sounding suddenly enthused. "We'll do it ourselves."

"Do what?" Finally, she was going to tell me why she'd called Edward.

"We're going to build a new room onto our cabin." She smiled at me. "We've lived in two tiny rooms for long enough."

"Really? That's great! Last winter almost drove me crazy, being stuck inside during that cold snap."

"I know. Me too."

"So how do we do it?"

"The old fashioned way. We don't need boards and nails.

27

We have lots of trees in the forest that have died or been blown down. We'll use them and make a log addition."

"*Log* addition?"

"Yeah, we have a saw and an axe."

"Saw? Axe?" Okay, so I sounded a bit stunned, but I just couldn't picture my mom swinging at a tree with an axe. A five foot four lumberjack. Right.

"Yes, saw and axe," she repeated slowly, as if talking to a toddler.

"Just so I know I heard you right," I persisted. "Us. Saw. Axe. Then us taking said saw and axe and cutting down… *trees*?"

"No, not you. Me."

"But I want to help too," I said, quickly turning on my whiny voice. Ridiculous as it all was, I wanted to be involved.

"Maybe a little. But I don't want you to hurt yourself. And remember, I am awesome. And heroic."

Throwing it back in my face, and so soon! "I don't remember saying that."

She laughed. "I know what I heard. And you're right, by the way. I am quite awesome."

Okay, so no wonder I'm just a little bit sarcastic at times. I get it from my mom. "So is Edward bringing us any nails?" I still didn't see how we could do a whole addition without nails.

A tight expression constricted Mom's face. "Edward can't help us."

"Why not?" Though I pretty well knew why not – but hearing it from her would confirm what I'd gathered from the phone call, plus it would give Mom a chance to tell me something, for once.

"I don't really want to talk about it right now, Evy. And besides," she added resolutely, "this is a blessing in disguise. It'll be educational and we'll be far more proud of it when it's done. I think we should put it beside the living room area, with the door connecting near the stove. That way, it'll be warmer in the new room at night."

"What's the new room for? A real studio?"

"It would make a fantastic studio, don't you think?" Her voice actually sounded dreamy. "There'd be a lovely view of the lake on one side, the meadow on the other."

I didn't mention that to have a view, we'd need windows and that they cost money. She didn't need to hear that just when she was starting to feel better.

We rounded the corner and our tiny cabin appeared, nestled on a rise. In front of the cabin, the land rolled down a gentle slope to a wild meadow and in back it sloped down to a small lake, the source of our water supply. A few trees stood around the small building, offering a bit of shade in the summer and a small protection from the wind in the winter. Our barn, where Rusty, Cocoa, and Twilight lived, sat at the side of the meadow, and that's where the horses headed, completely ignoring the house.

Their delight and anticipation rose as we rode nearer,

and it was a light, humming feeling. They could hardly wait for the yummy oats and hay, and the relaxing pleasure of the grooming they knew I'd give them after their long day.

We dismounted outside the barn and I held out my hand for Cocoa's reins. "I'll take care of her." Evening was one of my favorite times of the day and I wanted to be alone with the horses so we could talk.

"Thanks, Evy. I'll get dinner started. Don't be too long."

I watched her walk toward the house, her stride fast and strong. There was no longer any sign of the bad news she'd heard from Edward today. Good thing I'd eavesdropped or I'd have no clue what was happening. It was hard to be too mad at her though, because I knew why she was keeping this secret. She was protecting me. She didn't want me to worry. But how could I not? If people stopped buying her paintings we might be forced to leave our home so she could get work somewhere else, and that would be terrible.

What would happen to Rusty, Twilight, and Cocoa if we had to leave? Could they go with us? Horses are considered a luxury in most parts of the world. If we lived somewhere else – okay, *anywhere* else – they would no longer be a necessity. They'd become a hobby; a hobby I knew we wouldn't be able to afford.

Rusty bumped me with his nose. "Yeah, buddy. I know. Lots of lovely oats." I led the three horses into the barn. They'd done a good day's work and deserved all the nice things I could give them. Relaxing into the horses' satisfaction of a day well lived, my worries started to fade.

People can learn a lot from horses. For one thing, they tend to not obsess about what might be, preferring to deal with things as they happen. Plus they're amazingly open creatures. There's none of the twisted stuff where you feel admiration, irritation, and frustration toward someone all at the same time, as I sometimes feel with my mom.

I felt my body unwind and move into the rhythm of our nightly rituals with relief. Right now, I wanted to enjoy being with my uncomplicated, truehearted friends. I wanted to give them food and groom them, one by one, and listen to their calm thoughts. I wanted to relax with them. Such a heavenly idea.

But that meant no more thinking about those dastardly, infuriating secrets, and even more, about the terrifying, life-changing events they might contain.

The next day was uneventful, except that Mom got out
her axe and saw and spent the afternoon sharpening them.
Thankfully, I wasn't there for most of that exciting event.
I'd done my homework that morning, and so the afternoon
was free. I wasn't going to waste it hanging around the
cabin. Rusty, Twilight, and I decided to ride to Cartop
Meadow, a wild meadow about an hour's ride from home,
with a mound that looked like a massive car near one end
of it. I'm not sure why we chose Cartop – no reason, I
guess, except we wanted a nice long ride together – but
was I ever glad we'd chosen it once we got there.

Twilight was the first to notice the wild horse and she
knew not to spook him by neighing a greeting. Instead, she
showed her excitement by tossing her head and prancing
in a circle, her hooves silent on the soggy ground. When I
stopped Rusty, Twilight stopped too, then stared down at
the dark colt grazing near the meadow's edge.

I recognized the black-bay colt immediately, and no doubt Twilight did too. Dark Moon. He was a member of Twilight's herd before she came to live with me, plus he was her half brother. Their dams always seemed to be squabbling and biting each other, but Dark Moon and Twilight had gotten along. Now, he switched his tail and shook his mane, trying to keep the surrounding cloud of mosquitoes from settling on his body. He ate the fresh spring grass greedily and I was happy to see that he wasn't super thin anymore. Last winter had been pretty tough on the entire herd, Twilight included.

I searched the rest of the meadow but saw no other members of the herd. Unless they were all crowded behind the mound, they weren't here. I knew what must've happened. Dark Moon had probably been forced from his herd. Night Hawk, the herd sire, probably thought the three-year-old was old enough to be independent. Poor Dark Moon. His would be a lonely existence until he found a group of juvenile males to hang out with or he started a herd of his own.

As far as starting a herd of his own, there were only two ways he could do it: beat a herd stallion in a fight and take his herd by force, or steal mares whenever and wherever possible. Sadly, I knew Dark Moon would have to be a stealer; he might be big and strong enough to best a herd stallion, but he wasn't aggressive enough unless the other stallion was really old or sick. Even if he stole a mare or two, he'd have a tough time keeping them from other stallions unless he gained some confidence. In the horse world, it's not always the biggest and strongest who wins, it's the one who thinks he's the biggest and strongest.

Twilight started to inch through the tree trunks toward him. He was still some distance away and seemed totally preoccupied with his lunch and the mosquitoes, so she was able to get closer and closer. She stopped at the tree edge for a moment – I could feel her savoring the anticipation – then she leaped out into the meadow.

Dark Moon shot into the air and when he hit the ground, his legs powered him forward. Twilight raced after him. He'd almost reached the trees on the other side of the meadow when he must have recognized her, because he arched into a wide turn and galloped back toward her. They met and sniffed noses, squealed, struck with their front legs, and then sprinted away, side by side, with clumps of mud soaring up behind them.

Do not worry, my Human. I will return.

I smiled. Twilight doesn't have any trouble remembering horse names, but then the names that horses give themselves actually mean something in their world. The word "Evy" means nothing to a horse, so she still occasionally calls me her human.

Realizing I would be waiting a while, I dismounted and loosened Rusty's girth. Then I leaned back against a tree to watch the two young horses play while Rusty settled in for a good snooze.

Twilight and Dark Moon ran around the meadow three times, bucking and leaping, twisting and kicking, before they slowed. Then they played a rearing game, and finally they sidled up beside each other and gnawed on each other's withers for a while. After about half an hour of that, they stood side to side, with their heads and rumps reversed, and swatted each other's mosquitoes.

Time ticked along and the horses' minds quieted. I closed my eyes and relaxed into Dark Moon's feelings: he was thrilled to be with Twilight again. He missed her and Ice, his main playmates when he'd been in the herd. And he loved that he had someone to swat the mosquitoes from his face again. Tapping into his emotions, I felt so safe and cozy that I must have drifted off.

Wake!

I woke with a start. Rusty was looking off in the distance and Twilight was grazing beside Dark Moon in the meadow below. Evening was coming on. I had to get home soon or Mom would be worried.

Twilight didn't look remotely ready to go. Of course, I could always just show myself to Dark Moon and frighten the young horse away, but I didn't want to do that. The problem was solved when the wild colt raised his head, stared in the direction that Rusty was already looking, and snorted. A split second later, he spun on his heels and raced for the trees.

Twilight looked after him, and when he paused at the forest's edge, she neighed. He stared at her for a long moment, wondering why she wasn't running from whatever he'd sensed, then he dove into the forest and was instantly lost to shadows.

Twilight neighed again, and when there was no answer, she meandered toward us, stopping now and then to grab a mouthful of spring grass. I quickly tightened Rusty's girth and mounted, and the two of us strolled down the hill to meet her. I was curious about what Rusty and Dark Moon had noticed.

Have fun? I asked Twilight as Rusty and I entered the meadow.

Fun!

"Hello!" A man's shout came from the trees.

Twilight startled into a short run, skidded to a halt at Rusty's side, and crowded against him, her eyes large. I leaned down to slip her halter on her head, then turned Rusty to face the man and horse emerging from the forest across the meadow.

I gasped – I couldn't help myself. The horse was so amazing, so breathtaking, that I couldn't look away. Strong, proud, red as flame. A lump lodged in my throat. Both brave and beautiful horses do that to me; make me want to cry. I reached out with my thoughts. I had to speak to him…

"Hello," the man called again and my thoughts snapped back like a rubber band. Ouch! I forced my gaze from the magnificent chestnut, whose muscles rippled like water beneath crimson silk, and instantly

I recognized the man. Charlie, the guy who thought I looked like trouble. Great. Of all the people to come across, I had to find the only one in the entire universe who was already suspicious of me.

"Hi," I said, reluctantly.

He asked his horse to lope the last few yards and Twilight shrank behind Rusty as the big chestnut came near.

The gelding slid to an effortless, supple stop. "What are you doing out here?" Charlie asked.

Irritation loosened the magic his horse held over me. Like what I was doing was Charlie's business. "I live out here," I said in a snooty voice.

He almost seemed amused. "No. You live an hour's ride away, with your mother."

I barely kept my mouth from dropping open in shock. How did he know us? I certainly didn't know him, and I was sure Mom didn't either.

"So, again, what are you doing out here?"

"Who are you?" I said in such a way that he'd know I was really asking *who on earth do you think you are, asking me questions that you have no right to ask*?

"I'm Charlie Black, the new Wild Horse Ranger. My job is to watch over the mustangs. I make sure they're not being harmed." His eyes sought Twilight, still hiding behind Rusty. "And I make sure they're not stolen from the wild… like that filly. I recognize her and I remember her herd."

I felt the blood drain from my face. "Twilight wants to be with me." I tightened my reins and Rusty stepped back, eager to leave the tense situation. "She chose to live with us."

Charlie just shook his head. "That filly should be in the wild, with her kind. You can't just take horses from the herds on a whim."

"I... I have to go." I spun Rusty away from him and we trotted toward the trees with Twilight crowding Rusty's heels.

"The filly should be returned," he called from behind us. "You have no right to keep her! I'll come get her when I've located her herd!"

Instead of answering, I asked Rusty to gallop. We raced across the rest of the meadow, slowing only when we entered the forest. At the top of the rise where Rusty and I had watched Twilight and Dark Moon play, I stopped just long enough to unclip Twilight's lead rope. We could go a lot faster without the two horses tied together.

We loped and galloped the rest of the way home and made it there in record time. But even in the barn, cooling down Rusty and Twilight, and then feeding and grooming all three horses, I couldn't shake a horrible feeling of dread. Charlie saw us yesterday at the store and immediately recognized Twilight as being one of the exclusive Nemaiah Valley mustangs. He knew she was a wild horse, and as the Wild Horse Ranger his job was to protect the wild horses. If he had been telling me the truth about who he was, then he had to help her, or do what he *thought* was helping her.

But maybe he'd give up if I kept her in the barn for a few days, though Twilight would hate being locked up. Maybe he wasn't a persistent fellow.

Right. He'd ridden all the way out there looking for her the day after he saw her in town. It was probably a safe assumption that he was the bulldog type.

I could think of no way to convince him I hadn't stolen Twilight away from her family. He'd never believe why she was with me, even if I told him, which I certainly was *not* going to do. No one knew I could talk to horses and I definitely didn't want Charlie Black to be the first. But if I didn't do something, he'd come back.

I couldn't do *nothing*. But what *could* I do?

That night, I was a wreck, so focused on my problem of what to do about Charlie that I could hardly eat supper, let alone carry on a conversation. Luckily, Mom didn't notice. She was so into planning the addition to the cabin that she hardly knew I was in the room. She'd not only sharpened the axe and saw, but had marked some dead trees and windfall near the cabin that would make good log walls, and insisted on showing me every single one before it got completely dark. Loonie – that's our ancient German Shepherd – didn't know what to think with all the excitement from Mom and the worry from me. She kept switching between eager leaps of joy and sad-eyed drooping melancholy as she followed us around.

I was relieved, and I think Loonie was exhausted, when we went back inside. Mom immediately became distracted by her survival books that gave instructions on cabin building. Yeah, they do make books like that, and I think she has every single one of them.

After I went to bed in the bedroom that I share with Mom, it took me forever to fall asleep. What was I going to do if Charlie tried to take Twilight away from me? Was there any way I could stop him?

The next day I woke up grumpy, or at least I was grumpy according to Mom, who seemed excessively cheerful to me. Mercifully, it was Kestrel's day to come over, so I knew I'd soon be away from Mom's perky home-addition preparations. I still didn't know what to do about Charlie, so I pinned my hopes on Kestrel. Surely she'd have some ideas about what to do. She knew him better than I did, plus she could tell me if he really was the Wild Horse Ranger, or if he was trying to steal Twilight from us to sell or something.

I told Mom that I was going to meet Kestrel, then saddled Rusty, freed Twilight to run beside us, and headed out. If I was lucky, I'd get there before she left. I love hanging out in her room. It makes me feel like an average teenager, lounging on her bright comforter, talking, and listening to music. We *all* enjoy hanging out at Kestrel's, actually. While I relax and pretend to be normal, Rusty grazes in one of their massive pastures, and Twilight plays with Kestrel's dog, a sable collie named James. They have this competition going where he tries herding Twilight as she tries to chase him. It's hilarious watching them go in circles, faster and faster and faster. What isn't so funny is when one gets frustrated and tries to take a chunk out of the other. As you've probably already guessed, Twilight is usually the one to start the biting.

A rifle shot popped in the distance and I pull Rusty to a halt. "Whoa, buddy." He sidestepped nervously. "It's okay." I reached to pat his neck.

Danger, Twilight. Come near.

The filly spun around and ran toward me, but before she reached me another shot rang out.

Whoosh!

It didn't take a rocket scientist to realize that the whoosh was the bullet whistling past my ear!

"Hey!" Instantly angry, I screamed as loudly as I could. "Horses and people are right here!" I felt like adding, "You stupid idiots!" but thought it wouldn't be smart to provoke someone with a gun.

While the distant gunfire hadn't stilled the birds my shout did, and in the void left by their silence I heard an engine fire up. The motor revved and then roared away. It was an ATV, I was sure. And the shooter was fleeing.

I patted Rusty with a trembling hand. That was sooo close! To hear the bullet whistle as it passed us? How far away could it have been? One of the horses could've easily been injured or killed. Or I could've been. And judging by how fast that ATV took off after I yelled, I doubted they'd have offered any help. They would've just skedaddled as fast as their little machine could carry them, even if they'd hurt me or one of the horses. Jerks!

Then I heard it again. A motor. My heart thundered. Had the shooter heard the rage in my voice? Maybe I'd made him angry and he was coming back.

Rusty tossed his head. He didn't need to say what he was thinking. I knew we should get out of there.

I leaned forward over his neck and he sprung into a fast gallop. *Come quickly, Twilight,* I called to the filly, and moments later she surged past us and raced down the rough road in front of us. We'd be safe closer to Kestrel's house. She didn't live as far out in the bush as we did.

The motor's roar grew louder. Was it catching up to us? No! It was on the road in front of us!

I pulled Rusty to a sliding halt – *Twilight, come back!* – a split second before the green truck rolled around the corner. For a moment, wild panic blinded me. I'd been wrong about the motor being an ATV. It was a truck! And the shooter was… was…

Familiar? There was something about the way the driver held the steering wheel as if he was trying to throttle an attacking wild beast. And I'd seen that grimace before, that flash of white teeth grinding together. The last confirmation was the lettering on the truck that said it was a rental.

The driver was the only person who *ever* came to our house other than Kestrel and her family. Edward, Mom's agent.

Twilight was already high-tailing it back to us, panic sparking from her like lightning.

Safe now. Stay close.

Though she was terrified of the big green machine, she stopped and pressed her trembling self into Rusty's flank. Edward brought the truck to a screeching halt, then flung the door wide and lurched from the interior, his face almost as green as the truck. These roads, if they can be called roads instead of wide trails, can be pretty hard on travelers, especially reluctant ones.

"Hi, Edward," I said, leaning down to pat Twilight reassuringly on the neck.

"Evy," he gasped. Then he bent, put his hands on his knees and stared at the ground.

"Rough trip?"

No answer as he fought to control his travel sickness. I waited. Finally, he straightened. "Where are you off to in such a hurry?" he asked nonchalantly, as if moments ago he hadn't been almost puking his guts out.

"Nowhere. Just out for a ride. So how was your trip?"

He nodded, still a bit green. "Good, good," he said unconvincingly.

"You look a little pale."

"It's a long drive."

I couldn't argue with that. He must have left yesterday, stayed over in Williams Lake, and then left Williams Lake awfully early to get this far by mid-morning.

"So your horse had a baby?" he asked, motioning to Twilight.

"No, she's from the wild herd," I said, rather than

46

remind him that Rusty was a boy and would make a very strange dam.

He fidgeted and his eyes wandered as if he was wondering what to say next. Then he smiled. "Hey, I got something for you." He leaned back inside the truck and I heard a bag rustle. He emerged from the truck with two candy bars in his hand. He handed one to me, then leaned on the truck hood and opened his bar's wrapper. He looked at the exposed chocolate for a moment, then lowered it. "So your mom is painting horses now?"

"Yeah. They're awesome paintings too. You'll love them." I took a big bite of the candy and closed my eyes in ecstasy as the sweetness filled my mouth. This was heaven!

"I'm sure I will." Such positive words, considering his tone of voice sounded like he'd just stepped in cow poop.

"So…" I said dreamily, thoroughly enjoying my chocolate, "What did Mom ask you to bring when she phoned you? Building supplies?"

"Yeah."

"And you couldn't because her paintings haven't been selling. Why haven't they been selling?"

Edward looked at me suspiciously. "If your Mom didn't tell you, I don't know if I should."

"Hey, Mom tells me things."

Rusty stamped his hoof and kicked his rear legs up in a little hop, throwing me slightly forward. Edward's eyes popped wide. Of course, I knew why my trusted steed was instantly upset. I was stretching the truth again. But Mom *does* tell me things, I justified to myself. She tells me things all the time: like what we're having for supper, what funny thing Loonie did, what I should tackle next for homework, and so on.

I shrugged nonchalantly – which wasn't easy since I was clinging to Rusty's mane in case he wasn't finished showing his displeasure. "You're right. She didn't tell me that," I said to appease Rusty. "But I don't think she knows. Did she ask you why they aren't selling?"

He sighed, took a nibble of chocolate, chewed, swallowed… and finally spoke. "No, she didn't ask me why."

"If you tell *me* why, maybe I can help her get inspired by something that will sell better."

He hesitated for a moment, his gaze judging me. "Okay, it's because the tourists are the main buyers and they want local Vancouver stuff. Ocean scenes, totem poles, that kind of thing. Try to get her to paint something like that."

"Sure," I said, though I knew it would never happen. Mom would never create a painting just so it could sell. She has to love her paintings, every single one. "But mustangs are cool. Maybe they'll like wild horses."

"Maybe. I hope so." He turned back to the truck cab, the forgotten chocolate bar still clutched in his hand. Obviously, our conversation was over.

"I'll ride Rusty back to help unpack the stuff," I offered.

"You go first, then," he said. "The truck will be slower than your horse." He opened the door and flinched, as if he dreaded getting back inside.

I turned Rusty toward home. I'd have to go hang out in Kestrel's room another day. Edward only came twice a year and I wanted to see what he'd brought. There were always things missing from the list Mom sent him, but he'd add new stuff to make up for the shortfalls. Once he even brought jellybeans instead of popcorn. That was a great day until Mom discovered the candy and sent it back with him when he left, and then we didn't have any popcorn for six months.

Rusty moved stiffly beneath me.

Why are you still angry? I spoke truth to him, I told Rusty as we rode.

You spoke tricky at first.

I quickly changed the topic. *So fun to see what Edward brought.* Rusty didn't reply.

My upset gelding carried me back home while Twilight loped alongside, slowing only when we reached the cabin. "Mom!" I called, and listened. No answer. Quickly, I slipped from Rusty's back, hurried up the porch steps, and opened the door. "Mom?" Nothing. As I walked down the porch steps, Edward's truck roared up to the cabin. Moments later he was out of the cab and we both heard the call from the forest.

"Timber!"

I spun around in time to see a dead treetop tip sideways

into the forest and disappear. Mom was already felling trees. As Edward backed the truck up to the front of our cabin, I mounted Rusty again, gave him an apologetic scratch under his mane, and asked him to lope toward the forest. Twilight followed like a golden shadow.

"Mom!" I called again.

"Over here!"

"Edward's here with our stuff!"

"I'll be right there!"

I turned Rusty back and Twilight galloped away to do a kicking, bucking, snorting loop of the meadow. I hardly watched her as I hurried back to the cabin. If I was lucky maybe I'd have time to eat another candy bar, if Edward had more, that is. I didn't want the reject one that he couldn't eat.

He did have another. The second one wasn't as good as the first, but it was still plenty good and was gone way too fast. I reluctantly swallowed the last bite as Mom approached us, looking like a miniature, old-fashioned logger with her axe over her shoulder. She shook hands with Edward and welcomed him to the cabin as if just two days ago she hadn't been extremely upset with him.

"I can't wait to see these mustang paintings, Laticia," he said to Mom. "Evy's been bragging about them."

"Well, come inside. I'll put on some coffee too."

"Great."

I slipped off Rusty's saddle and bridle and plopped

them on the ground. I'd put them away later. Then I patted Rusty on his sleek gray shoulder and ducked my head. *Sorry.*

Rusty nuzzled me and his acceptance and affection flowed serenely into my mind. I drew in a deep breath. I hated it when he was mad at me, even when I pretended not to. Now, everything felt right again.

Inside the cabin, Mom put the first painting on the easel for Edward to view – Ice Dances, that's what she called it. It was a stylized painting of Twilight with Snow Crystal and Ice, two of the wild horses, dancing in the snow beneath a full moon. The ice crystals they kicked up surrounded them in a glittering fog, making them appear magical. It truly was one of Mom's best. I could tell that Edward was impressed as well. He stood with his chin in his hand, trying to act indifferent, but I could almost touch the excitement rising from him.

"Not bad, Laticia," he said. "Let's see another one."

She showed him another of the horses galloping across a frozen lake. And then another of our meadow, with the snow, peacefully untouched and inviting. And then there was the one with Twilight looking out from the barn. This one still made me feel sad. Vibrant longing was alive on her face, and though the viewer wouldn't know what the filly was looking at, I knew. Mom started that one when Twilight was still being held captive, when she still yearned to return to the wild. Mom had completely caught the absolute hunger for freedom in

Twilight's eyes and I still felt guilty looking at it. I was the one who'd caused her pain back then.

She put up the remaining two paintings, one of a Whiskey Jack in the willows at the edge of the lake, looking all blurry and misty and unworldly. She'd called that painting Spring Spirit. And finally, one of Cocoa and Rusty grazing together. This painting exuded comfort, two old friends completely at ease in each other's presence.

After each painting, Edward nodded and said something like, "Hmmm," or "Not bad."

Yeah, right. He was thrilled. I could totally tell. He just didn't want Mom to know it, for some strange reason. And oddly enough, she couldn't tell that he was completely awed and blown away by her paintings. She's kind of blind when it comes to her own work, and of course, she won't take my word for it that they're awesome.

"They *may* sell," Edward said in a doubtful voice when she finished showing all six paintings. "You want to help me unload? I should head back." Not another word about the brilliant paintings. I would've kicked him if Mom hadn't been there.

"Sure," she said, sounding disappointed. "Come help us, Evy."

The three of us relieved the truck of its load: box after box of canned goods and powdered things, and bag after bag of rice, beans, flour, sugar, salt, oats, and so

on. Some boxes were super heavy – my schoolbooks.
I couldn't wait to open those. One big box was light
and didn't rattle. I guessed it contained the new clothes
we'd purchased from the mail-order catalogue. I hoped
the sizes were right this time. After Edward's last visit,
I opened my clothing box to find that almost half of my
new t-shirts were too small. I ended up trading them for
some of Kestrel's clothes. She's smaller than me so she
fit the smaller T's, and I fit into some of the hand-me-
downs from her older sisters.

When we reached the bottom of the load, Mom turned
to Edward. "What's this?" she asked, pointing at the
plywood stacked beneath the heaps of supplies.

"I thought I'd help you out a bit, Laticia. You said
you needed building supplies. You can pay me for
them when these new paintings sell. I mean, if they
sell."

Mom seemed to both shrink into herself and grow
bigger as she put her hands determinedly on her hips.
"We don't accept charity, Edward. You know that. And I
don't buy anything on credit."

"But, Laticia, you need –"

"We need nothing. We'll get by just fine, thank you."
And she meant it, I could tell. Though it would be
awfully nice if she did accept the plywood. How else
were we going to make a floor for our addition? "If the
paintings sell, then we'll buy some plywood, *if* we still
need it," she added.

Edward shrugged, smart enough to not argue with her. "Whatever you say. Let's get the paintings packaged up."

The paintings were ready to go within minutes. Edward and Mom loaded them into the front of the cab, and then put our boxes of recycling into the back of the truck for Edward to take to a depot in Vancouver. He stayed a scant five minutes afterward to have a quick cup of coffee, then jumped into the truck, and rattled out of the yard.

The silence he left behind was deafening. Mom and I stood on the porch, staring at the muddy tracks leading away from the cabin. We were alone again, not counting visits from Kestrel, for six months now. At least that's what I was thinking. Not Mom. After a moment she sighed and put her hand on my shoulder. "I hate it when they leave. It's like sending off my children."

I hoped that she'd fight a bit harder to keep me than she did to keep her paintings, but in another way I was glad she'd told me. Mom hardly ever tells me anything personal. It's like she pretends to be iron-woman, totally invincible, with no feelings of sadness or confusion or anything negative. It wasn't until I was seven that I even realized she *must* have bad feelings sometimes, though she never talked about them.

"They're going to make their new owners happy," I said in an effort to cheer her up. "And I'm sure they'll sell too, Mom. They're the best you've done."

She smiled bravely at me, took my arm, and led me

toward the cabin door. "So let's see what Edward forgot this time."

"And what extra he put in," I added, hoping that there'd be a couple more candy bars or some other surprise. If I found them first, Mom wouldn't throw them into the stove to get rid of them – or so I hoped, anyway.

Kestrel arrived a couple hours later. I showed her my new books, which were awesome, and new clothes, some of which were too *big* this time. I was still happy, though. At least I'd get to wear these outfits. I just had to grow a bit more first.

Once when we were leaning over a box, pulling out food supplies to put away, Kestrel elbowed me. When I looked up, she pointed at my Mom's retreating back. Mom was sneaking into the bedroom with one of the boxes. From what I could see of it, it was big, and the furtive way Mom carried it made me think *birthday present*. I grinned at Kestrel. As usual, Mom would put it under her bed and maybe, just maybe – okay, honestly? For sure we'd take a peek later when she was busy.

Rusty's long, disappointed face flashed into my mind. I felt immediately irritated with myself. This was getting bad; I was even fantasizing his disapproval now. With an imaginary Rusty acting as my nagging conscience, how was I ever going to learn anything in this house of secrets?

That afternoon, when we went out to see the horses, Mom had another surprise for me, or actually, for Twilight. A new yearling halter. I was overjoyed because the halter Twilight had been using was so stiff that it wore bald spots on her cute little face, even when she only wore it when necessary. The new halter was bright green nylon and soft as can be. Twilight looked fantastic in it, though she didn't seem to like it as much as Kestrel and I did. She never has understood the need for halters and ropes, thinking that she can take care of herself. And she can, in the wild. It's only everywhere else that she's always getting into trouble.

That evening, we looked through the new catalogue that Edward had brought and I started thinking about what clothes I'd like to order before his next visit. There was no rush – I'd have six months to pick them out – but it was fun. I tried talking Mom into letting me order a beautiful white sundress, but she said no. When I persisted, it became a firm NO, followed by words like impractical, hard to keep clean, and winter wear. Apparently, I only needed jeans, T-shirts, and warm sweaters. Totally boring.

To make it up to me, Mom made caramel popcorn, which I adore. We stuffed our faces and drank hot chocolate, and did lots of laughing and running around, until Mom got sick of us and sent us outside, even though it was dark. We decided to make the best of it and asked if we could have a fire. She said yes, and soon joined us at the dancing campfire in a much better mood now that we weren't breaking things inside the cabin.

In all the excitement, I forgot all about the bullet whizzing past my head, and when I finally remembered, after we'd all gone to bed, I decided that it wasn't important and there was no need to worry anyone. The shooter was probably long gone and hadn't been shooting at me anyway. It was an accident and there was no harm done. One thing I definitely did though; I asked Kestrel if Charlie was the Wild Horse Ranger, if the job even existed. She hadn't heard anything about Wild Horse Rangers at all, but said she'd ask around.

The next day, we rode back to Kestrel's house with Twilight running before us in her luminous new halter. I got to do the coveted hanging out in Kestrel's room while Rusty ate and Twilight did whatever. Kestrel showed me a unicorn necklace and some other stuff that she bought in Williams Lake, then we watched a DVD. I felt so normal that I hardly knew how to respond when her sister Mya came into the room and told me that Twilight was chasing the new calves and their mothers were trying to gore her. I went out to save Twilight from the livid horned beasts, realized it was almost mid-afternoon, the time I'd told Mom I'd be home, and decided to forego the rest of the movie. I'd just have to come back soon to finish it, that's all. I went back inside to say goodbye to Kestrel and her family, answered a few questions from her mom about our new addition, and walked out the kitchen door with the distinct impression that they were all, except Kestrel, just a little relieved that I was leaving and taking my bratty filly with me.

I was close to home, riding peacefully along and thinking how strange it was that Twilight creates so much friction in my life, between Kestrel's family and me, Charlie and me, and in the past, Mom and me, when I heard another gunshot. Distant. Not whooshing past my ear.

Could it be the same shooter?

Another shot. And another.

It sounded like the same kind of gun.

I listened carefully but there were no more shots. What should I do? Go see what was happening? Or would that just be dangerous and stupid? Maybe I should continue on toward home and tell Mom.

No, I had to find the shooters now, while they were still nearby, and talk to them. By the time I rode the rest of the way home, found Mom and she got Cocoa ready, they might be somewhere else, still shooting, and causing a lot more problems. Like if they moved closer to our cabin. Not many people knew there was a tiny cabin beside the small lake; they might think the area was a safe place for target practice. And that's what they had to be doing. There was nothing else to fire a gun at right now. It wasn't hunting season. And what if a bullet struck one of the horses? Or my mom? She planned on being out in the woods a lot these days, cutting down trees.

I mind-called Twilight and clipped the lead rope to her fantastic halter, then the three of us headed off the road and into the forest, toward the sound of the gunfire. In order to not travel in circles in the bush, I picked out a distinctive lump on the low mountains before us, then every time we came to a clear spot I made sure we were heading toward that lump. We detoured around the thickest brush and avoided the lowest branches.

Twilight was grumpy about both being on a lead rope and struggling through thick forest. She wanted to run and play and be free, and she didn't mind telling me all about her dissatisfaction in vivid detail. The distant gunfire was nothing to her, a curiosity at most, and she wasn't the least bit frightened. I didn't want her to become frightened either, so I didn't tell her what guns and bullets could do. Some things are too hard to explain, especially to horses. They don't understand why any creature would want to kill another.

We'd traveled steadily for ten minutes, and I was just wondering if I'd chosen the right direction when we heard an ATV fire up to our right.

"Hey!" I shouted, hoping they'd hear me. I asked Rusty to lope and he wove through the trees like a pro. If I could just get within sight of the machine or machines, they might see me waving and stop.

We broke out of the trees into a swampy meadow in time to see two ATVs rumble toward the trees. But I didn't wave to stop them. No way. In fact, I heartily wished and hoped and prayed that they wouldn't look back and see me, because of what lay between me and them. A dead moose. Or more accurately, a dead moose with its head chopped off at its shoulders. So sick. Disgusting. Cruel. I felt nauseous even looking at it.

I forced my eyes away to stare after the ATVs. The forest green machines were big and muddy, and each carried one man. The ATV in the lead had a big dark brown and red blob tied to its rack. The moose's head.

Trophy hunters.

This was no legal trophy because it wasn't hunting season. And the moose was a female, a cow. It's illegal to kill cow moose *any* time of year. Plus, she wouldn't even make a good trophy to hang on their wall – her fur would be clumpy from spring shedding. These poachers couldn't be from around here. They were the worst kind of hunters: disrespectful of the laws, uneducated about wildlife, unaware of the life cycles of the land, and from the look of it, the type to shoot at anything that moved. In another word, *dangerous*.

The ATVs disappeared into the forest without the two men looking back. I glared after them, as close to hating someone as I've ever been. What total rejects! What miserable losers! Tears blurred my vision, and I turned Rusty away from the carnage. There was only one thing to do; go home and tell Mom. It was too late to save the poor moose on the ground, but maybe we could prevent any more from being killed by getting the authorities out here. Somehow, I had to talk her into going back to town.

Then I heard the rustling. Rusty stopped short and Twilight jumped back, yanking against the end of her rope. Their dark ears strained forward and both horses peered at the thick bushes to our left. The bush moved. Something was pushing its way through the wall of growth. A strange bleat emerged, and right behind it, a dark eyed, totally adorable, brown head… neck… shoulders… A baby moose! A very, very young baby moose. He looked only days old.

The cow had a calf that she'd hidden before the poachers shot her. The realization hit me like a sledgehammer and rage pounded through my body, filling me until I felt I'd explode. The poachers had killed more than just the cow moose. They'd killed this calf too, only his death would be drawn out as he starved to death or died from the cold; lonely, wretched, and filled with terror and confusion.

Unless we did something to help him. Unless we saved him.

We had to try.

The calf stumbled toward his dead mother, bleating
like a lost lamb. His eyes glazed over as he touched her
hindquarters with his nose. He didn't even seem to see us
watching him. Finally, he folded his thin front legs and
lowered himself to the ground, rested his too-big, graceless
head across her back, and closed his eyes. It was the saddest
thing I'd ever seen. He was waiting for her to wake up.

    We had to get him away from her body and back to
the barn. But how were we going to do that? By putting a
rope around his thin, fragile neck and pulling him along?
Taking him home on Rusty's back was impossible. I
wasn't strong enough to lift him into the saddle and then
get aboard myself and hold him there. But dragging
him along on the end of Twilight's rope seemed harsh,
especially since he was so obviously confused and
overwhelmed and miserable. But what other choice did I
have? I unclipped Twilight's lead rope.

The second she was free, the filly walked toward the calf. She sniffed at his back, then his head, and finally butted his side with her nose. He looked up at her, surprised. She butted him again, harder, and he scrambled to his cloven hooves and stepped toward her. She backed away and he followed, making sucking motions with his mouth. Maybe, since his mother wasn't moving, he knew enough to ask for help from another creature. Maybe he even thought Twilight was another moose, though she was lighter and smaller.

I reined Rusty forward to meet the moose calf, and while he sniffed the top of the calf's back the calf sniffed Rusty's front legs. Then the lonely little creature pressed close to Rusty's chest. Though the gelding was gray instead of brown, he was also bigger than Twilight and maybe that made the calf think even more of his mother.

I asked Rusty to take a step back and the calf followed. So I backed him another step and another, then turned Rusty toward the forest. We walked slowly into the forest, and to my incredible relief the baby moose tottered after us. We passed a few trees before the moose calf stopped. He looked back at his mother's headless body, bleated, and then tried to run back to her. But Twilight would have none of that. She jumped into his path.

Talk to him, she said to me. *Make him come with us.*

Moose don't understand me.

Try.

So I tried. The calf showed no outward sign of any sort that he'd heard, let alone understood. He just stared past Twilight with longing.

We have to get him to want to come with us, I told Twilight.

Twilight did the equivalent of a horsey harrumph and stamped a hoof. Then, with incredible gentleness, she bumped the calf toward Rusty with her nose. I asked Rusty to walk again and the calf reluctantly followed for a few more yards before trying to turn again.

Repeat this about a hundred times and we finally reached the road. After that it was easier. The calf was getting used to following us, and now that his mother's body was far away he felt more dependent on Rusty and Twilight. An agonizing hour later we straggled into view of our cabin. I led our pokey group to the porch steps.

"Mom!"

No answer. She must be out in the woods.

"Loonie!"

I scanned the forests that rimmed the meadow around the house. Loonie's sharp dog ears would hear me.

"Loonie!"

The dark German Shepherd emerged from the forest, her big ears pointing toward the house. So that's where Mom was working now. Loonie loped toward us and I asked Rusty to canter across the meadow. We'd only gone a few strides when desperate bawling erupted from behind us. Rusty stopped. The moose calf was struggling after us, not wanting to let us out of his sight. I sighed and called again at the top of my overused yelling voice. "Mom!"

Loonie reached us just as Mom strode out from the shelter of the trees. I waved to her to come, then turned my attention to Loonie and the moose calf. The calf didn't seem any more disturbed by the dog than he had been by the horses, which meant he was too young to have learned about the danger of predators. If we hadn't decided to investigate, he may not have died of cold or starvation. He may have ended up being some carnivore's dinner.

Mom held her axe in front of her as she approached the young moose, almost as if she wanted to protect herself. She doesn't trust moose much, apparently not even cute helpless ones. "So this is why you're late," she said. "Tell me what happened. Where'd you find it?"

I shook my head in disgust. "You won't believe it. Some creeps wanted a trophy moose head for their wall, but didn't know enough to not shoot a cow moose in the springtime." I couldn't keep the outrage from my voice. "It was the sickest thing I've ever seen!"

"The poor little thing." She slowly laid the axe on the ground and advanced on the calf. He accepted her presence as easily as he had the horses' and Loonie's. "They shot her right beside the road?"

"Well, no."

"So how did you know to go rescue him?" She scratched the calf on his shoulders and looked up at me.

Mom has a habit of asking the most irritating questions. There was nothing else I could do with such a direct question but confess. At least Rusty wouldn't be mad at me this time. "I heard the rifle shots and went to investigate." Might as well keep it simple and to the point.

She turned to me, incredulous. "You *followed* the sound of gunfire? Are you crazy?" That's the question always lurking in the back of her mind – is my daughter insane? It's a great confidence booster. Suddenly, she seemed to realize what she'd said. "I mean, what were you thinking, Evy? You could have been shot."

"I thought they were target practicing, and wanted them to know that we lived around here. I didn't want you or the horses to get hit."

Mom bit her lip, no doubt to stop the flow of words that were trying to shove their way out of her mouth. She took a deep breath. "Evy," she finally said, in her ultra-calm voice, "You *never* ride toward gunfire. Always come home and get me. Do you understand?" When I didn't answer right away, she asked again, just a bit sharper, "Do you understand?"

I nodded. I had to. Nothing could be gained by arguing with her, and besides, I would never be in this exact same situation again, right?

"We should get this little guy inside the barn. Good thing Kestrel came to visit yesterday." Kestrel brings a gallon of milk and a couple dozen eggs with her every week when she comes.

"I can get him inside, if you want to get some milk," I said, already thinking ahead to where the little calf would live. He'd have to take Twilight's stall. It was the smallest, and since Twilight and Rusty got along so well, they could share Rusty's bigger stall. Rusty's stall had a door that opened to their outside pasture too and I knew Twilight would like that. In fact, she'd probably like sharing a stall better than living alone, though I'd probably have to remind them to not fight over the oats.

After riding Rusty into the barn, with the calf, Twilight, and Loonie following behind in that order, I slid from his back and opened Twilight's stall door. Twilight walked inside and rattled her grain bucket. I explained to her that she'd be staying with Rusty for a while and she almost skipped out of her stall. I hoped Rusty would be half as thrilled about sharing as she was.

Together, we directed the calf into the stall, then I put Twilight and Rusty in theirs, making sure the door to the outside was open. I gave them some oats, and the squabbling began.

I told them to share and they ignored me, both trying to eat from both buckets at the same time. I chided and reminded them to act like grown up horses as they rushed back and forth between grain buckets, desperate to not let the other get a bigger share. It would've been funny if it wasn't so irritating to be totally and completely ignored. Finally, I let Twilight out of the stall and carried her oats toward the barn door. She stepped on my heels all the way, and the second I put the bucket down she attacked her snack with gusto. I stroked her golden coat as she chewed rapturously and gazed out at the greening meadow.

Mom came out of the house with a deep pan of warm milk in her hands and we walked back to the calf's stall together.

"I hope he can drink it like that," I said, and then opened the stall door and closed it behind us. The moose calf staggered toward us, shoved his nose into the pan and almost knocked it from Mom's hands, then choked and blew milk out of his nostrils, covering both of us with snotty milk flecks.

"Gross." I jumped back. So did Mom.

The calf advanced, licking his lips.

"Grab him!" yelled Mom. She was already pressing against the closed stall door. The calf was eagerly reaching for the milk again when I flung my arms around his neck, barely restraining him before he re-attacked the pan.

"Think he's hungry?" Mom asked, sounding amused as she put the pan on the ground at his hooves.

"Just a little." Slowly, I allowed him to lower his head. His nose touched the warm liquid and I let go. Instantly, he shoved his nose beneath the surface again. He came up snorting and choking, then in frustration, struck out with a tiny front hoof. The pan went flying and milk sprayed across the calf, us, and the walls.

"We need a bottle," said Mom, putting her hands on her hips and frowning down at our gangly charge. "And more milk. That was a quarter of our weekly supply."

"We can get more at Kestrel's house, and they'll have bottles for their orphaned calves too. We can borrow one."

Mom picked up the pan. "I'll ask to buy one from them. I want to tell them about the poachers anyway."

"And on the way, I can show you —"

"You'll stay here. I don't want you anywhere near where people were shooting." She opened the stall door and we both stepped into the barn aisle. The moose calf tried to crowd out with us, but we shut the door in his face.

"But, Mom," I whined, hating that I sounded like a four-year-old but unable to stop myself. "You don't know where to find the dead moose." The baby moose wailed, sounding eerily like me, only louder.

"I don't need to find it," she said, her voice firm. "If anyone needs to know where the carcass is, they can come here and talk to you."

"But how long do I have to hang around home? It's not fair. What if they *never* catch the poachers?"

The calf bawled again, almost like it was copying me. Mom must have noticed the similarity too, because a tiny smile touched her face as she turned away. She strode toward the tack room. "You'll stay home until it's safe again."

I was about to say that it was never safe in the wilderness but clamped my mouth shut in time. No need to get her concerned about the everyday dangers, like stumbling across wolves or bears, getting caught in freak snowstorms, falling off horses and breaking legs miles from anywhere, and all those lovely things.

"No arguing," Mom added before disappearing into the tack room, as if she knew what I was thinking.

Grudgingly, I admitted to myself that she was right. Now wasn't the time for lengthy discussions. We had the calf to care for, and besides, I needed time to prepare an invincible argument. "You'll hurry, won't you? He's so young. He'll weaken fast."

She emerged from the tack room carrying Cocoa's saddle with the bridle draped over the seat. "I'll be back in two hours. I promise. While I'm gone, you can try the pan of milk again, just in case he figures out how to drink it without spilling. Just don't fill it as full, okay?"

I nodded morosely and watched her saddle her chocolate colored mare. This was totally unfair – why should I be housebound because of the stupid poachers?

A minute later, Mom and Cocoa were trotting away from the cabin. They didn't look the least bit guilty as they left me behind. My jaw ached from clenching my teeth as they vanished around the corner.

I stomped back toward the barn. Rusty raised his head from where he grazed in the pasture.

You okay? he asked.

Yes.

Rusty's head dropped again. He flicked his tail at

73

mosquitoes as he munched, thoroughly enjoying the new spring grass. I looked around for Twilight, but she was nowhere in sight. Had she cut through the forest and joined Mom and Cocoa? I kicked the dirt. It wasn't fair. Twilight could go but I couldn't. Even Loonie could go. The dog had disappeared, so she must have followed Mom too. They'd both abandoned me. Deserters.

For a second, I thought of mind-calling Twilight before she got out of range and asking her to come home, but then I changed my mind. She'd probably refuse to come anyway, realizing it wasn't an emergency, and then I'd *really* be mad.

I sent a rock spinning away and trudged inside the barn. The moose calf was curled up in the straw, breathing so softly that at first I wondered if he was still alive. He looked so frail and melancholy that it hurt to watch him. He'd lost so much, the poor little guy – and here I was, being completely pathetic; complaining and whining to Mom about having my freedom restricted. The poor calf had lost everything, escaping with only his life. And he still might die, if we couldn't get food into him.

I meandered outside and toward the cabin, not in a hurry. The calf was resting peacefully, feeling safe and protected for the first time since his ordeal. A bit of sleep was probably good for him, as long as I didn't let him rest too long. A half hour would probably be the longest I'd want to wait before trying to feed him again – which would give me just enough time to thoroughly check out the birthday present waiting for me beneath Mom's bed. Maybe a little bit of snooping would make me feel better.

I put one foot on the bottom porch step and...

There's a whistling sound in the air and suddenly I can't breathe. There's something – a rope? A rope! – around my neck, tightening, tightening. I try to scream for help, but my wind is choked off. I run and hit the end of the rope – flip upside down. I hit the ground, hard. Still breathless. Can't get air. My body is shaking, quivering –

And then I shoved Twilight's terror through the back door of my mind and firmly slammed the door.

I came to, thrashing and convulsing on the wooden porch steps. My cheekbone felt like it had exploded, and I couldn't help but cry out with the intensity of the pain. Then I panted, groaned, and sat upright. Gingerly, I touched my swelling face, right below my eye. I'd knocked my face on the edge of the step when I lost control.

But I couldn't worry about that now. Twilight was in trouble; I had to save her. Someone had a rope around her and was dragging her away from our home. Was Mom in danger too? I reached out with my mind and touched Cocoa's. She was still within feeling distance, thank goodness. And all I felt was boredom as she trotted along. Major relief!

But Twilight was *not* safe. Cautiously, I listened to a whisper of her terror. I couldn't risk being carried away again. No, she wasn't with Mom. She was being dragged

in the opposite direction. Which meant no one but me knew she was in trouble. No one but me could help her.

I wasn't allowed to leave the cabin and yard, but right then, rules didn't matter. Twilight needed help and I was the only one who could save her. I'd deal with the consequences of breaking Mom's rules later, when my filly was safe.

I was halfway across the meadow when Rusty's thoughts popped into my head.

What is wrong?

I hate to admit it, but I'd forgotten about him. *Twilight in danger.*

I help too.

I turned back to the barn without bothering to answer, running as hard as I could. Twilight's panic was almost silent now, which meant she was swiftly being taken further from us. Soon she'd be out of range and then how would we find her?

I threw open Rusty's stall door. He trotted into the barn aisle and waited for me to jump on his back. I wasn't about to waste time with his saddle and bridle, so I leaped aboard.

Movement caught my eye. The moose calf was awake and staring at me. "Be back soon, Thumper," I said, the name coming from nowhere. Then I leaned forward on Rusty's back, clutched his long black mane, and we were off.

Though I couldn't hear Twilight anymore, I told Rusty to run in the direction I'd last heard her, then clung to his back with all my strength as he raced across the meadow. In the woods, staying aboard became infinitely harder. Branches ripped and tore at my hair, tree trunks flashed past just inches from my knees. I would have been swept off by low branches a million times if I hadn't been pressing flat to Rusty's back. Eventually, I had to ask him to slow down, despite the fact that Twilight was still too far ahead of us to hear. I just couldn't hold on any longer at that speed.

Rusty switched to a steady gallop and we traveled in the same direction for ten minutes without another peep from Twilight. Had they changed direction? Were we running farther away from her rather than closer?

And then I sensed her. Still terribly afraid. Still fighting the rope as she was dragged along.

We are coming, I told her and I felt her grow calmer, felt her stop fighting so much – and as a result, the capturing horse and rider moved her faster.

Slowly, so slowly, we gained on them, mile after mile. And finally I saw her golden rump moving through the trees ahead of us. And right in front of her a fire red horse. A stooped rider. Charlie. Just as I'd guessed.

"Hey!" I yelled, all my frustration and anger raging through that single word.

He stopped his horse and looked back. His eyes narrowed as we approached.

"You can't take her! She's mine," I yelled. Rusty slid to a stop beside Twilight, and the filly immediately cuddled up against him, shivering, her eyes wide and glassy. White rimmed.

Charlie looked down at Rusty, but didn't seem the least bit impressed that we'd caught up to him or that Rusty wasn't wearing any tack. "The filly belongs with her herd. You know that."

I clenched my jaw so hard, it hurt. This guy thought he knew everything when really he had no clue about anything. "She belongs with me and Rusty. It was her choice to stay with us. We didn't force her."

He shook his head dismissively, then asked his horse to walk on.

STOP!

The gelding catapulted into the air, wild eyed and snorting. He landed with all four legs spread apart and stiff, and then froze, not knowing which way to run. Charlie instantly put his hand on the gelding's neck and spoke to calm to him.

Okay, so I shouldn't have mind-shouted at the poor horse. This wasn't his fault. He was just doing what he was told.

Twilight gave the equivalent of a horsey mind-giggle,

then she pulled back on her rope again. Thankfully, the noose had a safety on it so that it couldn't tighten enough to seriously hurt her.

Stop fighting the rope, Twilight. I will talk to him.

The filly stepped forward, breathing heavily. The rope around her neck loosened.

"She chose to stay with us and I can prove it," I said. "And if you're really the Wild Horse Ranger, you'll let her go when you see she wants to live with us."

Charlie was still talking to his scared horse. I waited for him to respond, my anger slowly dissipating in the face of his horse's fear. I still felt terrible about scaring the poor thing. Can you imagine a strange language screaming suddenly through your head? The most stable of us would freak out and this big guy was no exception.

Finally, Charlie looked up at me. "So prove it," he said.

"You have to take the rope off her first."

Charlie shook his head, his eyes locked on mine.

"But how can I prove anything if she can't show you she wants to be with us?"

He shrugged, not caring in the least, and looked off toward the distant hills. "How long is this going to take?"

"Not long if you don't give me a chance to prove anything," I answered. "At least drop her rope."

Again he shook his head – but this time he gave Twilight some slack. Instantly, she darted to the farthest length of her tether.

"See? She doesn't like people," Charlie said as smug as can be.

"She likes *me*," I said and slid from Rusty's bare back. "I'll show you." I faced Twilight.

You want to escape?

Yes!

Do exactly – EXACTLY – what I tell you to do.

Okay. This was not said as grudgingly as usual. She'd do what I asked this time.

Come closer to the man. The rope will loosen.

Twilight hesitated for a moment, then stepped toward Charlie. The rope around her neck slackened.

Put your ears flat against your head… Now put your head down… Now shake your head!

The lasso slid neatly over her ears and landed on the ground.

"Hey," said Charlie.

Run in a big circle, I thought to Twilight, completely ignoring him. *When you come back to me, give me a kiss.*

My filly looked at me with a mischievous glint in her eyes, then spun away. She raced away through the trees, kicking and bucking. I crossed my fingers as her bum became smaller and even disappeared a time or two behind tree trunks and bushes.

"Looks like she's going back to her herd on her own," said Charlie, his voice swelling with satisfaction.

"We'll see," I said, hoping Twilight wouldn't feel tempted to hang out in the woods for a while, exploring and goofing off, her two favorite activities. If she didn't do what I asked her, Charlie was never going to be convinced. Of course I knew she'd come home eventually, but if Charlie didn't see her return of her own free will, how could I blame him for not believing Twilight had chosen us?

Twilight!

Do not worry.

I crossed my arms. Waited. Her running sounds became louder. Twilight sprinted toward us in a full run and came to a sliding stop right in front of me. She was breathing heavily as she leaned out and wiggled her lips against my neck. It tickled. I giggled. She did it again. I stepped forward and hugged her to stop her from tickling me. Then we both looked up at Charlie.

His mouth was open in astonishment. "How did you do that?" When he finished speaking, his mouth continued to hang open.

"Do what?" I asked, thinking he must mean some aspect of Twilight's training. Twilight's *training* – ha ha!

"Get her to trust you like that? How did you get her to leave her herd?"

"I… I don't know. I just talked to her, that's all," I said, stating the plain and simple truth. I'd had enough of Rusty being disappointed in me.

"It has to be more than that."

I just shrugged. What he thought really didn't matter to me, as long as he believed it was Twilight's own

83

choice to live with us. "So now you believe she chose us?" I put my arm over Twilight's back and we both stared at him.

"Yeah," he said, nodding his head.

I didn't bother hanging around for an apology, especially since the chances of getting one were slim to none. Charlie had done what he thought was right, just like I would've done if I'd been responsible for the wild horses. I was just relieved that now he believed Twilight had chosen us. And now I guessed he'd been telling me the truth too – he really was the Wild Horse Ranger. Otherwise, he'd still be trying to get Twilight away from me. So my conclusion about Charlie? He might be a grumpy guy, but he wasn't a bad one.

I jumped onto Rusty's back. Time to get home. Thumper had waited long enough.

"Hold on!"

I asked Rusty to stop. Since he wasn't wearing a bridle and he was anxious to start the miles back home, I was lucky he did. He turned to face Charlie, and threw his ears back. *This guy should go away.*

I agree, I replied. *Be patient. Do not bite him or his horse.*

Charlie rode toward us on his magnificent gelding. "She would've come back to you, even if I'd taken her the rest of the way to her herd. Why didn't you just wait for her to come back? Why'd you ride after us?"

Whew, an easy question. "You scared her. She didn't want to go with you and she trusts me to help her."

84

He looked at me thoughtfully. I was about to ask Rusty to go when the second question came flying at me. "You weren't there when I caught her. How did you know she was scared?"

I clamped my mouth shut.

"How did you know I'd even caught her?" he asked, sounding even more suspicious.

I could have told him that I'd been there, hiding and watching. I could have lied and incurred Rusty's displeasure – but even if I did, Charlie wouldn't believe me. The reason? The lie wouldn't make sense. If I'd been there when he first roped Twilight, why hadn't I stopped him then? Why'd I have to chase him halfway across the country to catch up to them? Obviously, I'd been far away when it happened. But I couldn't tell him the truth either. So I'd tell him nothing.

"We have to get home," I said and signaled Rusty to spin around. Faced toward home, he plunged forward. Twilight surged into a gallop beside us. A few strides on, we passed through an open spot in the trees and I glanced back. Charlie was watching us gallop away, a bemused expression on his face. Beside us, Twilight gave one last kick in defiance, then dropped behind Rusty and followed us back into the forest.

I felt Charlie's thoughts on us for a while, by way of his horse. Charlie's horse was picking up on his owner's feelings. He listened to Charlie's voice which was brusque and preoccupied. When the man patted his shoulder, the caress was distracted. Charlie Black was thinking of us – Twilight, Rusty, and me – and that gave me the chills.

If he decided to investigate, would he discover my gift, my life-long secret? I didn't think there was a way he could prove that I was different – but if he could, what would he do? What *would* I do?

All I knew for sure was this: *if* he realized I could talk to horses, and *if* he told Mom and Kestrel, it would change how they thought of me. It would make them treat me differently.

The situation was simple; I couldn't let him find out. I had to avoid him as much as I had to avoid those crazed, ignorant poachers, or maybe more.

I asked Rusty to slow down after half a mile and he was
more than happy to do so. He'd been out and about most
of the day and was getting tired. Not Twilight. I don't
think she ever runs out of energy. She bounced around
us, went on mini explorations, and pretended trees were
monsters until we were almost halfway home.

Suddenly, she paused, with her head high. She sniffed
the air. A moment later, Rusty and I smelled it too.
Smoke. He stopped before I asked him. Fire in the bush
was a super dangerous thing. It had been a dry spring and
a forest fire wasn't completely impossible. If we could
catch a blaze before it became too big, we might be able
to stop a forest fire and save many animals, and possibly
even humans, in the process. I knew the moose calf was
waiting for us. He needed us desperately. But to ignore
the possibility of a forest fire would put every one of us
in danger.

"Let's check it out, Rusty," I said, decision made. I laid my hand on the left side of his neck and he turned toward my touch. We trotted about a quarter of a mile with Twilight glued to Rusty's hindquarters and finally came to a ridge top. Before us, the ground dropped down into a large, forested bowl. A single column of smoke spiraled up from below. I saw a flash of blue through some trunks. A tent? Relief made me exhale and slump on Rusty's back. It had to be campfire smoke.

Go home? asked Rusty.

Not yet. I'm not sure what made me hesitate. Maybe it was my subconscious mind at work, telling me this was the perfect place for a hidden camp. Maybe something seemed wrong or out of place, or maybe I'm just really smart… ha ha! Okay, honestly? It was my mom who made me hesitate. I heard her voice in my head, droning on and on in one of the *millions* of campfire safety lectures that she's given me over the years.

We should make sure the campfire is safe, I answered Rusty. I didn't see anyone down there. The campers might be hidden by the trees and brush between us, but then again, they might have left the fire unattended, and that was dangerous. If everyone was gone, we should put the fire out. No doubt it would make the campers mad to see a pile of dirt where their fire used to be, but that was better than them starting a forest fire with a stray spark. They'd thank me if they knew what they were risking.

Because I didn't want to make a preachy entrance in

case someone was just lounging out of sight, I left the horses on the ridge top with strict instructions to Twilight to stay put. She looked at me crossly, then turned her head away.

Bossy, she said, and shook her mane.

So much for gratitude after saving her from the scary man. I leaned against Rusty's warm gray shoulder for a moment and gave him a hug. Twilight was still ignoring me, so I headed down the hill with no more displays of affection. I'd be back in a minute, I told myself.

I went as quietly as I could. That way, if someone was there, I could turn around when I saw them and they'd never know I'd been sneaking up on their camp. When I was halfway down the incline, the sun dropped behind the higher land. I was surprised. It must be later than I thought. I glanced at my watch. Oh my! It wasn't just late afternoon, it was *very* late afternoon. Mom would be back home soon – if she wasn't already – and she'd be way beyond furious to find me gone.

I scrambled back toward Rusty and Twilight, only to stop short after a few yards. I really did need to check that the campfire was safe. There was too much at risk – all the wild creatures' lives, including Twilight's mustang herd, our little cabin and barn, *us*. I was just going to have to be tough and risk getting into mega-trouble.

I hurried back down the hill toward the camp, and as I descended a far-too-big campfire came into view. Three tents surrounded the merry blaze; two were fancy, bright

blue, and new, and one appeared to be homemade with old canvases. Items were strewn about the campsite. These campers were messy. A food cache hung in a tree to keep it safe from bears. Nowhere did I see people. The only things indicating that they may not have gone far were the two mud-caked ATVs parked near the fancy tents, forest green ATVs that looked suspiciously like the poacher's ATVs.

I stopped. What would the poachers do if this was their camp and they found me here? Poaching was highly illegal. They'd have to pay huge fines if they were caught. Jail time could even be involved, especially for their guide. If they caught me, they certainly wouldn't let me go, because once I'd seen them I could identify them.

I turned and was about to bolt when reason caught me. Even if they saw me, they wouldn't know that I knew they were poachers. They'd think I was just an ordinary kid who thought they were ordinary campers. They'd have no idea that I'd seen their ATVs before or that I'd found the dead moose.

Silently I crept the rest of the way down the hill and slid behind a tree, then peered out to see inside the rustic tent directly across from me. It was empty. The fancy tent on the right had its door zipped shut, but I could only see the back of the second tent. Someone could be inside, staring out at the flames.

I slid along the side of the tent, my heart racing like a runaway horse. My breathing was so shallow that after a few steps I felt dizzy. I bent over, put my hands on my knees, and waited for the feeling to pass. Obviously, I didn't have a future as a gifted spy. Finally, I made it to the front corner, and slowly, so slowly, leaned around – to see the door was zipped shut. So I was safe, unless these losers were having a nap, in which case they'd be asleep. I straightened, inhaled deeply and quietly, then prowled toward the campfire.

The heat it gave off was amazing. It really was much too big to leave unattended. They must've dumped a stack of wood on it before they left. Only dirt would kill this fire quickly. I had to find something to scoop with.

My eyes wandered the campsite, searching for anything with a wide flat blade. The interior of the homemade tent looked promising with its jumble of objects just inside the door. That's where I'd start looking. I hurried toward the disorganized mess and… that's when I heard them. Voices, coming from my left and getting louder. At least two men were walking toward camp and talking to each other.

I froze, all my brave thoughts instantly gone.

Hide!

The two new tents were too small but the big ugly one, with its canvases and poles and handy little rips for peepholes, was ideal. I raced behind it, realizing too late that it was also the farthest from my escape route to where Rusty and Twilight waited.

Behind the tent was a large lump covered with a worn

blue canvas. Flies buzzed around it. I crouched down next to the smelly thing hoping that whatever it was, it wasn't something the campers needed while I was hiding.

Obviously I wasn't thinking clearly. I bet you can guess what was splayed beneath that canvas. My only excuse is that sheer terror addles the brain.

The two men laughed as they entered the camp, then continued to chat in a language I didn't understand. I leaned forward to peer through a hole in the ratty tent. The men were still talking as they went to the fire. One was medium height with graying hair, while the second was younger and taller. Their faces looked kind of the same, so I guessed they were father and son.

The son dropped an armload of wood and then threw some more sticks on the blaze, while his father balanced a big pot of water he'd been carrying to one side of the campfire. The flames grew even higher. It wouldn't be long until the water was boiling.

I was about to fade back into the trees – I could climb out of the depression and then walk around the rim to where the horses waited – when the older man strode straight toward the tent I was hiding behind. I ducked down and held my breath. Seconds stretched past and I heard nothing but the crackling, popping fire. Had he entered the tent? Was he checking the perimeter of the camp? Maybe he was coming around back to check on the canvas-covered lump.

My body, demanding air, interrupted my morbid

imaginings. Slowly, I inhaled and the slight sound
seemed unnaturally, terrifyingly loud.

Then I noticed that the food cache hanging beside
my ratty tent, thankfully on the far side of the lump
I hunkered behind, was being lowered to the ground.
Down, down it went. I flattened myself against the dirt,
willing myself to blend in despite my purple jacket. In
mere seconds, the older man would be bending over it,
removing something, and all he would have to do is look
to his left and I'd be caught.

The food cache hit the ground. The man stepped into
view, leaned over it, and opened it. I wanted to close my
eyes, but I couldn't. If he saw me, I had to run. There
was no way I could pretend I'd just happened across
their camp now, not when I was crouched behind this…
whatever it was. My gaze shifted to the canvas lump.
With my swollen cheek pressed against the ground, I
could see under the edge of it, and an eye was looking at
me. A large, dark, glazed over eye.

It took all my strength to not scream. Or maybe it
wasn't strength but simply self-preservation and fear of
what might happen if I got caught. It's amazing what a
person can do when they have to.

I stared into the eye.

It stared back.

The man at the food cache straightened and turned
to his companion, his eyes passing right over me. The
younger man yelled something from the fire and his

father yelled back, then stalked out of sight with a jar of instant coffee in his hand.

Tears sprung from my eyes and I reached under the canvas to touch the rough hair of the cow's face. The poor thing. She'd died to feed vanity; her head would hang on a wall and these men would brag about killing her to their friends. And just as heartbreaking, she'd left behind a baby that she'd never see grow up.

But he *would* grow up. I could promise her that. I'd take care of him and teach him and do the best I could to replace her, so he would become a strong young moose that she could've been proud of.

Shaking like crazy, I moved to watch through my peephole. The father stood impatiently over the water as it heated, as if he thought staring at it would make it boil faster. The son poked the fire with a stick. They were talking softly, almost furtively, to each other in their own language.

Suddenly, the younger man shrugged, then dropped his stick and strode straight toward my tent! I jerked back, my heart roaring in my ears. I was going to die of a heart attack if I didn't get out of here. And then the roaring got louder. And louder. Another ATV, probably the guide, was approaching the camp.

I moved back to my peephole in time to see the man who'd been striding toward the ratty tent quickly step back to the fire. He picked up his stick and poked at the blaze far too nonchalantly. I couldn't help but smile. It looked like he'd planned to do some snooping in the guide's tent and had been thwarted.

Do not let anyone see you, I sent to Rusty and Twilight. *They are the poachers, the one's who killed Thumper's mother.*

Thumper? asked Twilight.

The calf, Rusty guessed.

Yes. Be careful. Cannot talk more now. I needed to be aware of what was happening around me. I felt Rusty lead Twilight away from the noise of the ATV, and ached to sneak up the hill and follow them. The two poachers were completely distracted, turned toward the sound of the ATV and waiting for it to come into sight. It was the perfect time, except I couldn't leave yet. I had to see the guide too, so I could describe him to the authorities.

The third ATV roared into camp with one person aboard. He came to a sudden stop beside the fire and turned his machine off. The silence seemed surreal after all the racket.

"So I found another one, a young bull," the guide said as he dismounted the machine.

The young man rubbed his hands together and grinned while the older guy scowled. Apparently, the father had already got his poached moose: the cow. The bull was meant for the younger man. Not that the bull would look much different than the cow. It would have the same ratty tufted look about it and only stubby new horns. Moose re-grow their horns every spring and lose them in the fall, and a young bull moose would have even smaller stubs than an older bull moose. These poachers were totally clueless, and they were being taken advantage of by the guide who no doubt knew all this stuff. They were probably paying a lot of money for this expedition too. If I wasn't so mad at them for killing Thumper's mother, I would've felt sorry for them.

I stared through my peephole as the three men talked about their plan to "bag" the bull the next day, the two foreigners in stilted English. I strained to hear every word. I needed to memorize as much as I could about the three men, including their conversation.

After listening for less than five minutes, I turned to make my escape through the forest at the back of the worn tent. Evening was coming on quickly. Mom would be insane with worry by now, probably imagining me lying wounded and lost in the vast forests, and calling out for her with my last breath.

I crept a few yards into the forest, only to close my eyes in dismay and freeze stock-still a second later. A shout. Not telling me to stop. The poachers still hadn't seen me. And they weren't yelling at each other either. No, this was a new person – a familiar person – calling down to the camp, letting them know he was approaching.

Charlie.

I slid, silent and swift, back down the hill. If I waved
at him from the tent corner as he approached, to warn
him, maybe he'd leave without asking the poachers any
suspicious questions. Judging from how Charlie was with
me, he wasn't very good at talking to people and would
probably say the wrong thing.

I peeked around the edge of the big tent. There he was,
riding his amazing horse into the poacher's camp. I was
about to wave when a new thought made me hold back.
What if I was wrong about Charlie? What if he wasn't a
Wild Horse Ranger, but really one of the poachers? If I
waved and he was one of them, I'd be so caught!

And then he was past me and approaching the fire.

Quickly, I moved back to peer through my favorite
peephole. The two poachers were shifting nervously and
staring into the flames, while the guide simply looked
scared to death. Charlie had stopped his horse, and – oh,

oh – I recognized that expression on his face. I'd seen it too often, directed at me. Intense and obvious suspicion. In another way though, I was relieved to see it. It meant he wasn't one of the bad guys. Now, if he could just play it cool…

"Hello. Name's Charlie," he said, and nodded a stiff greeting.

"Martin," said the guide. "What brings you out here, Charlie?"

"Just checking on a mustang herd in the area and smelled the smoke. Wanted to make sure everything was okay."

Martin relaxed, just a bit. "Everything's fine here. We're keeping an eye on it. But it's good of you to check." His words didn't match his tone. He wasn't the least bit pleased that Charlie was doing the right thing. "You better be heading out soon. Night's coming on."

Unfortunately, Charlie seemed to hear what I heard: the unspoken impatience. The barely veiled fear. His eyes narrowed further. "Mind if I have a bit of that coffee first?"

Martin hesitated, then turned back to his ATV. "Help yourself." He pulled a small daypack off of the back.

Charlie's saddle creaked as he dismounted his gorgeous horse. "You got a cup?"

"Inside the cache," said Martin and stalked toward me, or rather his tent. I jerked back and hunkered low, breathed quick and shallow through my mouth. Listened. Martin rustled around inside the tent.

"You fellows from around here?" Charlie asked.

There was no answer from the two poachers, and I imagined them both shaking their heads, no. I guessed they wouldn't want Charlie to know they had accents, so even though they knew English they wouldn't speak.

I heard Charlie walk toward the cache to get the cup – or I hoped it was Charlie. If it was, I had a second chance to warn him. But what could I do to signal the whole story to him. Pantomime a hunter shooting a gun? Pretend I was a dead moose?

Charlie came into sight and bent over the cache. He pushed some stuff aside, pulled out a cup, straightened, and then noticed me waving frantically from behind the tent. His eyes opened wide. "Huh?" The exclamation was soft, but in the woods, things don't need to be very loud to be heard.

Quickly, I lifted up the canvas to show him the gory moose head. Understanding flooded his eyes and he looked quickly back at the fire, then let the cup drop back into the cache and stepped out of my sight.

"You're right. It's getting late. I better be going," Charlie spit out, clearly angry. "Thanks for the offer of coffee."

I cringed. They were going to know he'd seen the moose head. He'd have been much sneakier to drink their coffee, make innocent small talk, tell a joke, and then leave. I'm the backwoods girl who only talks to her mom and best friend and even *I* know that.

"Why the rush all of a sudden?" Martin sounded more

than scared now. He sounded mean. I risked a glance out my peephole, just in time to see Martin step between Charlie and his horse, while the old poacher grabbed the reins. The young poacher moved to the side, his eyes on the ground, and for a second I was reminded of one of those dogs who sneak up behind you before they bite you.

Charlie and the guide faced each other like two bull moose. Of the three men, the two poachers and the guide, the guide had the most to lose if he were caught: his money with fines, his freedom with jail, and his reputation with his friends, if he had any friends. Not only did he have a lot at risk, but he was bigger and younger than Charlie. He probably thought that grabbing the old guy would be easy. I guessed differently. Charlie was probably more stubborn than the lot of them.

But he was outnumbered too. And that was his undoing. As Charlie glared at Martin, the younger poacher slipped unnoticed behind him. I would have yelled to warn him and then run off into the woods as fast as my legs could carry me, but the guy was so quick that he had both of Charlie's arms pinned behind him before I could react. Then Martin sprang forward and grabbed one of Charlie's arms.

Run! I mind-shrieked at his horse.

The horse reared, jerking his reins from the surprised poacher's hand, then spun away and sprinted into the forest, more afraid of the scream that had echoed through his head than actually obeying my command. The poacher started after him, even though he was obviously never going to catch the horse, but then stopped short when Martin yelled for a rope.

Charlie was strong. He made the poachers work hard to hang onto him, and it was no easy job tying him up either, but really he didn't stand a chance. Within two minutes, he was lying on the ground between my hiding spot and the fire with both arms and legs securely bound and the three men standing over him with red faces, breathing heavily from their exertions.

The son poacher glared down at Charlie, looking like he wanted to spit on him. "Now what we do?" he asked instead.

Silence followed his words as the three pondered the answer to the question, and then the father poacher spoke in a deadly soft voice, "We get rid of him."

My heart lurched.

Martin stepped back and his face drained of color. I waited for him to say something to stop them. Clearly, he didn't like the idea of getting rid of Charlie. Maybe he would give the poachers another option. Or defend Charlie. Or flatly refuse to let them hurt him. Instead, he said nothing as he stared down at Charlie with a blank, stunned face – and I saw that he was a coward at heart.

Cowards didn't risk themselves to save others.

But he wasn't the only one who could save Charlie. I could act too. I just had to figure out what to do. At the very least, I could run for help.

But what if they hurt him while I was gone? What if they moved camp or left the bush and Charlie was never seen again? What if…

Charlie sat up. He looked up at his captors, and though his back was to me I could imagine the sneer of disgust on his face. Then he did something that seemed totally un-Charlie-like. He scooted backwards a few inches, away from them.

There was no way he could escape, tied like a calf ready for branding, and they knew it. They ignored him as he inched backwards. So why was he doing it?

Then I understood. Charlie was doing more than inching away from them. He was inching toward me.

And I knew how to save Charlie.

Hello.

A spike of terror lanced through the red horse's heart and he froze, not knowing which way to run to escape the voice resounding in his head.

I am Evy, the human of Twilight. I am sorry for scaring you.

The horse snorted, then trotted in a circle, his step high and animated.

I need your help to save Charlie.

He stopped. Snorted again.

Listen to me?

He didn't speak in words, but answered in intent. *Yes.* He wanted to help Charlie.

Quickly, and in the simplest language I could formulate, I explained my plan, then added, *Wait for "go."*

Redwing, for that was his true horse name, agreed,

and so I turned my attention back to what was happening in front of me. The three men were arguing now. And Charlie was a lot closer to the tent. Thankfully, they were still ignoring him. It was time to make my move. Sweat beaded on my forehead even though the evening was cool. I could so easily get caught, and if I did – well, I didn't want to think about that.

I felt along the bottom of the canvas tent. I'd noticed that the tent floor was dirt, so something had to be anchoring the canvas walls to the ground. I found the first spike, and carefully, so I wouldn't shake the wall and give away my position, grabbed the top of the spike and tried to wiggle it. It was stuck fast in the earth. I moved on to the next one, just a foot away. I'd need to remove at least one spike in order to slide beneath the tent wall, and maybe two.

The second spike too was solidly in the ground. Again, I moved on. The third spike was the lucky one. It wiggled. I worked at it until it rose about an inch above the level of the ground, then took the round top in both hands and pulled straight up. The spike slid from the dirt as smooth as can be.

I hurried back to my peeking hole to see what was happening. Charlie was only four feet from the door of the tent now, his back still to me. The men stood beside the fire, discussing his future in intense, but quiet, voices. I wished I could hear something. Then I'd know how much longer I had.

Suddenly, the older poacher glared at Charlie. "Stop!" he yelled.

"That's far enough," added Martin, his face glowing in the firelight – and the difference in his expression from just five minutes ago really creeped me out. Gone was the indecision and reluctance. It was as if he didn't see a man anymore when he looked at Charlie, but an animal that he was hunting. His face was like granite, his eyes like ice.

I had to hurry.

I crawled back to where I'd removed the one spike. It's amazing how your mind clears when life is at risk. You just do what you have to do. I didn't bother trying to remove another spike. One would have to be enough. I wouldn't be able to slip through and escape as easily afterward, but if I didn't hurry I had no doubt that Charlie would be a goner.

I lay flat against the ground and lifted the canvas. A big backpack was right on the other side of the wall. I reached through and pushed it. It slid… and something on the other side of it fell over.

I froze. Martin would be looking at his tent. Striding toward me…

Charlie coughed. Was he trying to cover the sound?

"What was that?"

Charlie coughed again.

The following silence was absolute… and then, "I think it's better if we…" Martin's voice dropped again as he continued adding to their dastardly plan.

I breathed in. They thought the sound was made by Charlie.

Scrounging up my courage, I shifted the backpack a bit more, hoping, wishing and praying that there was nothing else to tip over. The backpack protected me from view as I shimmied under the worn tent wall and then army-crawled along the inside wall of the tent. Beside the backpack was a reeking pile of dirty clothes – how long had they been camping here anyway? From the smell, I'd say years! I passed it, holding my breath. And then I was at Martin's stinky old sleeping bag. There was nothing to hide behind now. I'd be in full view of whoever cared to look inside the tent. But there was no other way to get to Charlie, no way to get out of possibly being seen, and no time to do anything else but just go for it.

I was infinitely grateful it was getting dark. Maybe the shadows would offer some cover. Taking a deep breath, I slid along the stinky slippery sleeping bag like a river otter on mud, not daring to raise my head to look out the open door – and then I was at the far corner. My hand bumped a filthy pillow and I felt something smooth and cold beneath the softness.

Hmmm. What was this?

I held it before my eyes and smiled, then slipped it into my jacket pocket.

A second later, I was at the side of the doorway and cautiously peeking out. The men were still at the fire. Charlie was sitting ramrod straight outside the tent.

I guessed he was trying to become as big a barrier as possible to any malignant eyes that might see me creeping up behind him. I was glad he'd thought of it, and I imagined he was glad that I was here to save him. Without me, he'd be toast. In fact, he'd probably be so grateful that he'd never be suspicious of me again. If I hadn't been here – *Oh*... um, he wouldn't have *seen* the moose head, so he wouldn't have acted surprised and angry at the poachers, and they wouldn't have caught him or tied him up... Okay, so maybe I shouldn't expect gratitude when this was all over.

I got as low as I could and, totally zoned with an adrenaline overload, I belly-crawled out of the tent and along the ground toward Charlie.

Inches seemed miles.

Seconds seemed years.

Any moment I expected a shout or the stomp of angry footsteps or someone clutching my shoulder. It was agony. Pure, excruciating agony!

Unbelievably, I made it all the way to Charlie. With shaking weak fingers, I touched the knots binding his hands. Tugged. Were they ever tight!

I took hold again and picked at it... and picked and picked and picked. Nothing loosened. Charlie pushed his wrists closer together, trying to create some slack in the rope.

"So we agree," the young poacher said.

Now I wished I wasn't close enough to hear. I didn't

want to know the specifics of what they were going to do to Charlie, especially when they'd probably do the same to me if they caught me.

But they were all finished with their planning. The two poachers simply murmured in assent, and Martin said nothing. But why would he? It was his plan they were all agreeing to follow.

The first knot loosened.

There was the soft sound of a coffee cup being set on a rock.

The first knot slid undone, leaving only a trillion more to undo. I said a silent prayer that the old poacher would come up with a new inventive way to get rid of Charlie. I just needed them to talk for two minutes, that's all. I wouldn't even complain too much about one and a half.

"Okay, bring him here," said Martin, sounding meaner than a brooding hen. "Let's get this over with."

It's amazing how time can stand still when you're terrified. Everything moves in slow motion and I felt I was moving even slower than that once I heard Martin's words. Ten thousand minutes later, I'd inhaled once and heard the second coffee cup being set down in a long drawn out tone of metal on rock.

"Hhuuurrrrryyyyy," whispered Charlie.

Ggooo! I mind-shouted to Redwing, and the word pulled out long in my brain like a howl. I fumbled with the next knot.

"Heeeyyy!"

I'd been seen! I looked up to see the youngest poacher staring at me with shocked eyes.

"What?" asked Martin, spinning around, again in slow-mo.

My fingernail bent back as I jerked on the next knot and I cried out. But the knot loosened.

The young poacher took his first running stride toward us… and then they heard Redwing crashing through the bushes toward us. Fear careened instantly to all three faces. The running poacher slid to a stop and they all spun to face the sound. Was a hunger-crazed bear coming to eat their food? Coming to eat *them*? They didn't expect it to be Redwing, that's for sure. I had time now, mere seconds, but still better than nothing.

I undid the last knot just as Redwing burst into view and ran toward the group, his ears back and teeth bared. He looked powerful and vicious and glorious and luminously stunning, all at once. I would've cried at his beauty if I wasn't so scared.

Charlie's hands whipped forward to untie his legs. "Go," he said to me, and believe me, I went! I raced around the back of the tent and lunged up the hillside. I heard a raging horse cry behind me, and then someone shouted, his voice almost as high as a scream.

A gunshot exploded!

You two safe? I didn't want to stop. I was still too close to the camp, but I couldn't both run and concentrate enough to horse talk – and I had to know if one of them had been hit...

I waited. There was a long pause. Thirty seconds. Forty five. Fifty.

Safe.

I closed my eyes in relief, but only for a moment. I had to get safe too. I ran, crashing through bushes,

leaping over blowdown, dodging tree trunks. Halfway up the incline, I slowed to a jog to talk to Rusty. I didn't have to concentrate as much with him.

Rusty! Can you come?

Coming!

"There she is!"

I almost screamed. Only my survival instinct stopped me from wasting the time and energy. I charged up the rest of the hill, using my legs to run, dash, sprint, rush; my arms to grab branches and jerk, haul, pull myself along faster, faster, faster. I became mindless. I became panic. I became the ground I covered, the bushes that opposed me, the hill that stole my breath… On and on, up and up and up…

And then I noticed the sound of my pursuers – their thrashings, grunts, and rude exclamations – became just a little quieter. And a little quieter still. I was leaving them behind. There's something to be said for complete and total terror, that's for sure.

Then gold and silver flashed between the tree trunks in front of me. Twilight and Rusty! I ran toward them, slower now that my panic was dying, and flung my arms around Rusty's neck.

"Thank you, thank you," I gasped. "Thank you." His strength seeped into me, calming me. His awareness steadied me.

But he wasn't relaxing; his muscles felt iron hard beneath my hands. I turned and looked back. The young

114

poacher was about fifteen yards back, racing toward me with a crazed look in his eyes.

I jumped aboard Rusty's back – and suddenly I felt ridiculously safe. Even a little bit sassy. I know, I'm bad.

"Hey, bad guy!" I yelled.

He stopped to glare at me. Streaks marred his cheeks where branches had slapped him. I hoped they stung. I know it sounds mean, but he'd been willing to "get rid" of Charlie. Sure, I'd wanted to get rid of Charlie too, just a couple hours ago, but it wasn't remotely the same type of getting rid of.

"You are so busted," I added, and smiled at him, sweet as honey.

He roared and rushed forward. I couldn't help but laugh as Rusty leisurely spun about and swept into a canter, carrying me safely away.

I looked back once, just in time to see Twilight, who had lagged behind, kick her heels up in the poacher's face. The man skidded to a stop, his face bright red with anger. He clenched his fists as we galloped away. He knew he wasn't going to catch me now. They could chase us with their ATVs, but ATV travel requires trails and meadows, or at the very least wide spaces between trees. Horses could cut through the endless forests, and besides, it was almost night, which gave us even more of an advantage.

As soon as I was out of sight of the bad guy, the trembling started. No, I'm not a total freak – it's normal after having masses of adrenalin surge through your body. The trembling built and I had a hard time hanging onto Rusty's back, especially since he wore no tack and was determined to get me away from the poachers as quickly as possible. When he realized I was having trouble, he slowed down a bit. He's so thoughtful – or practical. No time would be gained if I fell off.

Then I noticed he wasn't heading straight home.

Where we going?

Redwing and his man.

We met them about a mile from the poacher's camp. Charlie's face was still gray from the aftershock of his experience and his expression was serious. He stopped Redwing in front of us and stared at me. I kept quiet, leaving the first words up to him, sincerely hoping they'd be words of gratitude and not one of the many accusations he could throw my way.

"You okay?"

I nodded. "You?"

"Yeah." Charlie sighed. He didn't sound overly thrilled about being okay. "I'll ride into town tonight and tell the authorities, but I don't know if it'll do any good." His forehead wrinkled. "All the guide needs to do is stash his ATVs and guns, dump the moose head, and then put on clean clothes and shave. They'd never recognize him from our description. We don't even have a name to give them. And unless the guide tells the police the names of his clients and where they're from, they'll never be caught either."

My smugness at bringing criminals to justice vanished in a puff of dismay. "I thought the guide's name was Martin."

"That wouldn't be his real name. He wouldn't be stupid enough to tell us his real name," Charlie said, sounding completely sure of himself.

"I know who he is."

Charlie looked up, suddenly interested. "You've seen him before?"

"No, but…" I pulled the wallet I'd found under the pillow from my pocket and held it up for Charlie to see. His eyes lit up.

I tossed it to him and he opened it, then grinned. "How'd you do that?" For the first time ever, his eyes smiled at me. He wasn't nearly as intimidating when he smiled. I almost relaxed. Almost.

"I came across it in his tent, when I was on my way to rescue you." Hint, hint, Mr. Ungrateful.

"Yeah, thanks for that. Takes a lot of courage to do what you did."

"No problem. You would have done the same for me." And I knew as soon as I said the words that they were true. Charlie would've done everything possible to save me if our positions had been reversed. Even though he had a suspicious nature and seemed grumpy the vast majority of the time, he was okay. And now that that was all settled, I needed to get going. I could feel Mom freaking out.

Charlie nodded, acknowledging the basic fact he would've saved me too. "So you can get home okay?"

"I don't need an escort, if that's what you mean."

He nodded again. But he didn't ride away. Wasn't it time for him to go? Didn't he have to hurry? But still he looked at me, the whites of his eyes glowing in the near darkness. I was about to ask Rusty to turn, thinking that Charlie was done speaking even though he wasn't going anywhere yet, when his voice floated toward me. "There's an old native legend my grandmother told me as a child. You don't hear it much anymore, but I remember."

A couple of frogs croaked in the silence that followed.

"Yeah?" I said, prompting him to hurry.

"The short version is that over countless generations people became removed from the earth, distant from all that is wild and natural, separated from their beginning. And so the great mother, in her wisdom, caused a bridge to be built between humans and animals."

A chill wind blew around me. It was almost dark, but I could still see Charlie's eyes and it looked like he was staring right through me. I didn't want to hear what he had to say. Like that was going to stop him.

"Within every human generation, one person is born in the gulf between the worlds," he continued. "This person understands both humans and animals, and acts as the bridge to the natural world for the rest of humanity." He paused and cleared his throat. "This person can speak both languages."

I could hardly breathe.

"I think," he added, his words as slow as molasses, "for this generation, the bridge is between human and horse."

"That's a stupid story," I managed to croak, but barely heard myself over the sound of my blood rushing through my ears. Of course, he ignored me.

"When I was a child, I wished I'd been born with the gift of speaking to horses. It was my favorite imaginary game – but just a game. But you?" He leaned forward in his saddle. "Well, there's no other way to explain Leo coming right when we needed him most. There's no other way to explain you winning a wild filly's heart, or that your gelding is perfectly controlled with no bridle."

"Let's go, Rusty," I whispered.

"Wait. I need your help one more time," he added, before we could leave. "It's important and only you can tell me. What is Leo's real name?"

"I don't know what you're talking about," I said, a little more firmly. There was no way he was going to trick me like that. No one would know my secret unless *I* told them. No one.

Charlie leaned back in his saddle and looked grumpier than ever. "Well, we both better be going then," he drawled and reined Redwing – no, *Leo*, I had to start thinking of him as Leo, or I'd mess up – away from me. Then he stopped, looked back. "Just one more thing. I respect your gift. Your secret is always safe with me."

Then he asked Leo to walk on. Within seconds, they were lost to the night.

I stared after them in a daze until the urgency of my situation forced itself back into my mind. I had to get home. Poor Mom would be freaking. I'd have to think up some story to put her mind at ease.

Once everything was done, once Mom was over her anger and the calf was saved, then and only then, could I fritter away my time thinking. Charlie thought he knew my secret. He guessed that I could talk to horses. The realization made me sick.

So my worst nightmare had come true: someone else knew. The big question was, what would Charlie do with that knowledge?

I heard Mom yelling for me long before I came in sight
of the cabin, her voice trickling through the tree trunks
like the cry of a lost soul. I yelled back, but she mustn't
have heard me, because she shouted my name again,
panic alive in her voice.

Rusty cantered nearer. I answered her call again.

"Evy?" she shrieked. Loonie barked uproariously.
Rusty loped in their direction, and then my mom and
Loonie came into sight, dark silhouettes among the trees.
Rusty stopped and I slid from his back.

Mom rushed forward to grab me, her hands like eagle
talons digging into my shoulders. "Are you okay? What
were you doing? Do you know how dangerous it is for
you to be out here? What if something had happened to
you?" All this in a very *loud* voice.

"Mom," I said, trying to break into her terrified tirade.

"Can you imagine how I felt, coming back here with

Kestrel, worried about escorting her here safely when there are poachers about, only to find you gone? *Gone*?"

"Mom!"

"I can't believe you'd do this to me. Taking off like that. What were you thinking?" She was crying now. She released my shoulders and stepped back. Now that she knew I was okay, her relief at seeing me safe was quickly turning to anger. "You must have known I'd be worried sick! How could you just take off –"

"I didn't leave just for fun," I interrupted loudly, hoping to stem her barrage of words.

"What?"

I drew a deep breath. "I didn't leave for fun. I had a reason. Right after you left…" I stopped, not because I wanted to but because I couldn't continue with the elaborate and extremely dumb lie I had prepared.

"So why did you leave? Where did you go?"

Emotions galloped through my head. Thoughts jostled each other. Mom was always doing this to me, hiding the truth. And how I hated it! So maybe it was time to stop doing the same to her. "I… I left because someone stole Twilight. I got her back –"

"What do you mean, someone stole her?"

"Charlie, that old guy in town who was watching us at the store? He's the Wild Horse Ranger and he thought she should be back with her herd." The truth tasted strange, but good, on my tongue.

"But didn't you explain to him?"

I started walking toward home and she turned to walk beside me. "I did, but it took a long time to catch up to him. He was going fast. He let Twilight go after I proved to him that she wanted to stay with us, but then, on the way back..."

Our feet crunched over the forest floor. Rusty and Twilight, tired of our slow pace, swept around us and trotted ahead through the trees. "But on the way back, I came across the poacher's camp."

She inhaled sharply but said nothing, allowing me to continue uninterrupted. We reached the edge of the meadow and stopped. I looked at our safe little cabin nestled on its small rise, dark because no one had lit the lanterns inside. Rusty and Twilight's shadowy forms trotted slowly across the meadow. Soft light streamed from the barn's open doorway. Kestrel must be with Thumper.

Tears sprung to my eyes. I loved our home. I loved the simplicity of it, the beauty of it. There was nowhere else I'd rather live, no other lifestyle I'd choose. No other people I'd rather have in my life. I stepped closer to Mom and she put her arm around me.

"What happened, Evy?" Mom asked.

And I told her. I didn't spare her anything, except the talking-to-horses bit. I even took a chance by telling her about Redwing rushing into the camp at just the right time to distract the bad guys and carry Charlie to safety. I told her the entire story as the moon rose behind the cabin, a long thin curve of silver.

Twilight and Rusty had been inside the barn for a full ten minutes when I finished. Mom said nothing.

Oats? Twilight asked.

Soon. I felt her stamp her hoof impatiently. I should get in there and settle them for the night. They certainly deserved the royalty treatment after today. But still, Mom hadn't spoken.

"Mom?"

She drew in a deep breath and pulled me even closer. It felt good. Warmer, too. "I don't know what to say." A shudder passed through her body. "So many things could have gone wrong. I could have lost you. And if anything happened to you, I couldn't live with myself. If I hadn't brought us out here, you wouldn't even know what poachers are."

"I'm glad you brought me out here. I don't understand *why* you did it…" I paused in case she wanted to volunteer some information, but she said nothing. "And I hope you tell me soon." Still no comment. "But I'm glad you decided this was where I'd grow up. Don't even *think* about leaving here because of those stupid poachers. They're losers. And I'm guessing it's just as dangerous, only a different kind of danger, out there in the cities, because of the things you haven't told me." I liked this truth thing. "Or haven't told me *yet*," I added firmly, letting her know, in a matter-of-fact way, that I expected her to tell me her secrets someday.

Mom cleared her throat. "It's just so hard to not be

there to save you, when you need saving," she said and wiped her eyes. "Or I should say *if* you need saving."

"I'm growing up. I don't need the same stuff."

Mom sighed. "Now that's a horrible, but true, statement. You don't need your mom in the same way you used to."

"But I still need her."

Mom put her other arm around me too and pulled me into a hug. "You're a great kid, Evy. Even if you don't understand how dangerous things can be. And you're incredibly capable. What you did today, well, that was amazing."

"It was kind of exciting, actually."

"Kind of?" Mom laughed. "Well, it's time for more excitement, with a moose calf who needs our help." She released me and we started to walk toward the barn.

"How is he?" I asked.

"Pretty far gone. He may not make it."

The lantern hung in the barn aisle and Rusty and Twilight stood by their stall door, one patient and half asleep, and the other extremely impatient and fidgeting. I hurried to Thumper's stall to see the moose calf resting his head on Kestrel's lap. His entire body was as limp as a soggy dishrag. Kestrel was leaning over him, trying to push the bottle nipple into his mouth.

"He's still alive," I said with relief.

Kestrel looked up, her dark eyes large in her face. "I can't get him to drink anything," she said in a desperate whisper. "It's like he doesn't even know it's here."

"Evy, wait. What's that?" Mom's hand was on my chin, turning my face. Oh yeah, the swollen cheekbone. "Did they… did they hurt you?" Her voice resonated with pure unpolluted rage.

"I fell on the porch stairs," I said quickly, glad it was the truth – though I would've lied about that no matter how disappointed Rusty would've been in me. Lied until tomorrow anyway. I didn't want my mom heading out into the night looking for poachers to beat up, and she sounded mad enough to do just that.

She exhaled audibly. "We'll put some cold cloths on it when we get in the house. And I'll take care of the horses. You do what you can to help Kestrel."

"Thanks." I stepped inside the stall, leaving the door ajar, and knelt in the straw beside the calf and Kestrel. His neck was warm when I stroked it, but he didn't open his eyes. "What can I do?"

"Maybe if you hold his mouth open, I can drip the milk inside," she said. She sounded devoid of hope.

"Sorry, buddy," I whispered and poked a tentative finger into his mouth. He opened one eye. A good sign, I thought, but then he closed it again. His jaws were slack as I pried them open. Kestrel squeezed the nipple and a tiny bit of milk streamed into his mouth – and dribbled out the other side. It soaked into her jeans, joining the other wet spots dotting her thigh. She'd been trying to do this for a while now.

"I'll tip his head back so it can't run out," I said.

She nodded and I lifted the moose's head so that his nostrils and mouth were poking up in the air. She squirted more milk into him and we watched it dribble down into the deeper recesses of his mouth. I put my hand on his throat. He didn't swallow.

"More," I said.

"He'll choke."

I looked into her tired eyes. "It's better than him dying." Which, if he did, would totally be my fault. There was no getting away from it. I'd abandoned him. Sure, it had been to save Twilight, but it didn't change the fact that I'd chosen her over the moose calf – and now he might die because of it.

Kestrel looked at me sympathetically. She knew me so well that she'd guessed what I was thinking. But there was no time to talk about it now. She tipped the bottle and sprayed more milk into his mouth.

"More."

She sprayed more. And still he hadn't swallowed. She gave him another good squirt and suddenly he spasmed, struggled, and coughed. Milk shot from his mouth and flecked our jackets and faces. Suddenly wide-eyed, Thumper lurched in panic, his long legs flailing as he struggled to stand. Then, just as quickly, he collapsed again, sprawling across both Kestrel and me. He rolled his eyes and gave a low moan.

Tears burned in my eyes, but I willed them away. Somehow, we had to get him to eat. If he ate, he'd be fine. But the poor thing looked like he'd given up. "Let's try again," I said, not knowing what else to do. Gently, I moved Thumper's head into position. Kestrel squirted the milk.

Straw rustled in the doorway of the stall; Mom had come in to watch. Kestrel squirted more milk into the calf's mouth. In case it might help him swallow, I moved his head gently back and forth, forth and back, one hand soft on his throat so I could feel if the milk went down.

"Girls, I think it's too late –"

I didn't hear the rest of Mom's sentence. Thumper swallowed!

"More," I said, trying to keep the excitement from my voice. Maybe it was just a fluke. Maybe it was my imagination, or wishful thinking.

Kestrel tipped the nipple into his mouth and squirted – and Thumper's tongue moved to catch the stream of milk!

"He's drinking it!" I said and Thumper opened his eyes. He pulled weakly to free himself from my grasp, and I slowly released him so he wouldn't flop over. His nostrils flared and he could barely hold his head above the straw, but he was moving on his own. His eyes focused on me, then Kestrel, then moved on to the bottle.

Kestrel knew what to do now. She'd fed literally dozens of tame calves. Wild babies wouldn't be any different. Within a minute, she had him sucking on the bottle, feebly to be sure, but still sucking. A lot of it dripped out of his mouth because he was so weak and not

used to bottles, but he was swallowing with every third pull. The level of life-giving liquid in the bottle lowered as Kestrel held it in place, and Mom and I watched with grins on our faces until the milk was half gone. Thumper stopped drinking as suddenly as he started. His nose bumped into the straw and his eyes closed. A second later, he was asleep.

We whispered and giggled like happy little kids as we snuck out of his enclosure, said goodnight to the horses, and blew out the lanterns. Our baby was asleep and we didn't want to wake him.

On the way back to the house, Kestrel and I devised a plan to care for the little mite. We'd feed him every two hours for the next day, at least, and for longer if he remained weak.

Kestrel and I couldn't decide who would take the first shift in two hours. We argued back and forth for a little while and finally agreed we'd do it together.

Because we needed extra rest if we were going to get up every two hours, Mom insisted we go to bed as soon as we finished supper. I admit I was beyond exhausted. I crawled into my sleeping bag near the stove, where Kestrel and I always sleep whenever she stays over, feeling like I'd just climbed Mount Everest. Mom placed a cold wet cloth over my throbbing cheek, and I closed my eyes and tried to relax.

Sleep, beautiful sleep...

But actually, *no sleep*. The day's events raced through my
head and then Kestrel, who, of course, wasn't as tired as
I was, started whispering questions. I told her all about
finding the moose calf and bringing him home, about
Charlie stealing Twilight and having to convince him that
she wanted to stay with us, and about the scary stuff in
the poachers' camp. The two hours sped by.

We continued our conversation during and after
the feeding, but Kestrel was finally getting tired too.
We fell asleep about half an hour before the midnight
feeding, and it was *sooo* hard to wake up. But we did it.
I stumbled around, heating milk and pouring it into the
bottle, and then watched Kestrel feed him. He slurped
and gulped noisily, and then drifted off again. Kestrel and
I tromped silently back to the house and climbed into our
sleeping bags. I'm sure I was asleep two seconds later.

The 2 a.m. feeding was even more arduous, except

that I came up with a great plan. Mom agreed, so Kestrel and I moved our sleeping bags out to the stall and crawled inside. Kestrel started to snore, and then the next thing I knew, someone was hitting me. At first, I thought Kestrel must've crawled out of her sleeping bag the moment my eyes closed to play a joke on me, but when I looked up a long furry nose was whacking me. Not Kestrel. Thumper. His dark eyes stared down, hungrily. I shone my flashlight on my watch. Only an hour and a half had passed. So much for my great idea. We were going to get even less sleep this way.

I warmed the milk in a pan on the little wood stove in the barn as the calf woke Kestrel.

"Leave me alone, Evy," she mumbled.

I snickered from the barn stove where I stirred the milk. Like I'd hit her while she was sleeping!

"Evy! Stop it!" Then she must have realized who was actually bumping her because she stopped yelling. She groaned and made a weird growling noise, then stood. She appeared over the stall partition with straw sticking to her everywhere, especially her hair. She looked hilarious and I was about to laugh and point when she started giggling. I looked down. I was covered with straw too. The pale strands seemed to especially like my new flannel pajamas. My hand flew to my hair to discover enough straw for a couple of birds to build a nest and raise a large brood.

This time, Thumper drank an entire bottle before falling back asleep, and I got to sleep for three and a half hours before he butted me again, this time much harder. Apparently, he was getting his strength back.

Again I warmed the milk while Thumper woke Kestrel. We were falling into a routine, except this time, before coming to the stove to fill the bottle, Kestrel walked over to the barn doors and peered outside.

"Is Mom up yet?" I asked her, guessing that she was looking at the cabin.

She looked again. "I think so. There's smoke coming from the chimney."

"I bet she's making pancakes for us."

While Kestrel fed Thumper I fed and watered the horses. There was grass in their pasture, but I wanted it to grow higher. And besides, we actually had hay left over from the winter. We needed to use it up before we bought the next year's hay from Kestrel's family.

When I returned to Thumper's stall Kestrel was already gone. Weird. She was usually as hard to pull away from the animals as I was.

"Evy, hurry up," she called from outside the barn.

"Wow, you're hungry," I replied, then gave Thumper a final head scratch. "Good boy," I murmured. "You're a tough little fellow, aren't you?"

As if to prove my words correct, he did a funny hop and jump, then started to explore his stall.

Deliciously, I was right – Mom *was* making pancakes, the best kind ever, with little bits of apple in them and lots of cinnamon.

"Those smell awesome!" I said when I entered the cabin, making Mom smile. I expected Kestrel to say something similar, and when she didn't I turned. She was still outside, looking down our driveway. Okay, so now this was just plain strange.

"Thanks," said Mom. "They're almost ready. Why don't you set the table?" I hurried to comply. The sooner the table was set, the sooner we could eat.

"Oh, yum," said Kestrel, finally coming inside. "Can I help?"

"Sure," said Mom. "We need the maple syrup and butter on the table too."

"Did you save the apple cores?" I asked Mom as she carried the delicious pancake mountain to the table. Rusty and Cocoa loved apple cores, and I assumed Twilight would too. She'd never eaten an apple in her life, so she might be a bit leery to begin with, but knowing her and her stomach, she'd quickly become addicted. Then she'd start rooting through everything, searching for apples.

On second thought, maybe the apple cores should go in the compost.

"So how are you girls feeling this morning?"

"Tired," Kestrel volunteered.

"I think we can wait longer between feedings now," I added. "He's getting strong fast, and I have the bruises to prove it." I shoved a huge forkful of maple-syrup-slathered apple pancake into my mouth and closed my eyes to enjoy my first heavenly bites.

"Bruises?" asked Mom.

I explained Thumper's ingenious method of waking us, which Mom thought was hilarious. Then her face became businesslike. Uh-oh. "I want you to tell me everything about yesterday again, Evy. Right from the beginning, starting with finding the moose calf, and I'll interrupt with questions."

I almost choked. This, during my heavenly pancake experience? I glanced at Kestrel – she was staring out the window. What was up with her? "But I'm hungry," I mumbled to Mom through my mouthful, then swallowed.

Mom smiled. "Okay, as soon as we're done then."

I took another bite, much smaller this time, so I wouldn't finish too quickly. Then I elbowed Kestrel. "What's happening? What are you waiting for?"

She looked at me, guilt all over her face. "What do you mean?"

She really needed to work on her innocent expression. "You kept looking outside when we were in the barn," I said. "And now you're staring out the window. You're waiting for something. It's obvious."

Mom looked up with interest, her eyes searching Kestrel's face. "Are your parents coming over today?" she asked.

Kestrel looked down at her pancake. "Don't make me tell you. I'm not allowed to say anything."

"So there *is* something," I said. "I knew it!"

Loonie barked and we all turned toward the big

window overlooking the meadow. Kestrel's horse, Twitchy, the only horse in the pasture, stared toward our rutted driveway, her ears forward. Loonie barked again, her "intruder alarm" bark.

And then we heard it – a vehicle. Someone was driving up to the cabin. A horse neighed, a horse I didn't recognize, and Twitchy replied. Then another vehicle approached, with a louder engine. It sounded like an army was arriving.

"You know who it is?" Mom asked Kestrel.

Kestrel nodded. "I was sworn to secrecy. I'm sorry."

Mom's face turned pale.

"But they've come for a good reason," she added.

"Who are *they*?" asked Mom.

"Mom, Dad, Caroline, and Jon, her son. The Robinsons; they have five kids. Troy and his brother. Troy was going to try to find Charlie too."

"And *why* are they here?" Mom sounded like she was about the have a heart attack.

"To help."

The truck stopped outside and assorted voices told Loonie to hush. Not that she would – the old girl was having too much fun. This was more people than had ever come to our house, multiplied about ten times.

"It's okay, Mom. Don't worry. These are just our neighbors and some people from town. They're not bad people."

Mom looked at me, and I saw fear in her eyes. Real

fear. What could our neighbors do to hurt her? "You don't understand," she said. "What if…" Her voice trailed off as she remembered not to say anything that might hint at her secret. I sighed heavily. A few more words could have told me volumes.

"I'm really sorry," Kestrel murmured again. She sounded like she was going to cry.

"It's going to be okay," I said firmly, trying to take control of the emotions swirling around Mom and Kestrel. "There's nothing to be sorry for, Kestrel," I said. "Right, Mom?"

Mom pushed herself up from the table, looking stiff.

"Right?" I repeated, when she didn't say anything.

She closed her eyes for a moment, took a deep breath, then opened them. "Evy's absolutely right. There's nothing to be sorry for, Kestrel. I'm the one who should apologize. You and your family are wonderful neighbors. I'm sorry I overreacted." She looked toward the door with dread.

"What're they coming to help us with?" I asked.

"The addition for your cabin. It was Mom's idea. She thought you'd like the help, so she went around to the other ranches yesterday. A lot of people said they'd come. They've all heard about you and want to be friendly, that's all."

"Awesome," I said. And it was. I was totally into visitors.

Another vehicle door slammed, and another horse whinnied. I reached out to the new horse with my mind – it too was a stranger. And so were the four other horses being ridden into our yard. So Charlie hadn't come. I hoped he'd made it to town in time for the police to catch the guide and poachers last night, but maybe he hadn't.

Someone knocked at the door. I looked at Mom and she nodded, then arranged a smile on her face. She was going to make the best of it. I was proud of her. If she'd freaked, the entire experience would've been destroyed.

Now I could enjoy this day to the max. Having this many people over was almost like a party. And my birthday was in just a few days. Thirteen years – yay!

Within minutes, we'd met everyone and Mom was even laughing a little, the tight lines in her face relaxing more with each passing moment.

We unloaded the trucks of windows and boards and nails and other mystery items, and then Kestrel and I took the brood of Robinson kids and Jon, who was our age, with us to care for everyone's horses. It was fun watching their seven horses, plus Twilight, Rusty, and Cocoa, run around the meadow playing. Twitchy was the only one not interested in play, instead hanging out in the shade and pinning her ears back whenever anyone got close to her.

However, Twilight thought it was great. She was used to living in a wild herd and loved the camaraderie of a large group. One of the horses, Lane's I think, was only three years old, and after all the horses settled down and were grazing, Twilight and the three-year-old continued to have as much fun as possible. They kept ripping around, bucking and kicking, spinning, dancing, cavorting – basically doing any and every wild leap imaginable. I caught Mom watching them a time or two and wondered if she was getting an idea for a new painting. I hoped so. I'd love it if the horses inspired her again.

When it came time to feed Thumper we took all the kids with us. We had lots of helping hands, that's for sure. The youngest Robinson, a two-year-old girl, was so cute. "Tumpoo, tumpoo," she kept saying, after we told her the calf's name. Then of course, everyone started calling him Tumpoo. They took turns holding the bottle and feeding him as the chainsaws roared outside.

Once or twice I snuck away to peek at the house, but there wasn't much to see other than everyone milling haphazardly about. Mom was right in there too – and she was smiling. I was too far away to tell if her smile was genuine, but her laughter sure sounded real. She seemed to be talking to Elaine and Caroline a lot, which I thought was great. I wasn't lying when I said my mom needs some friends.

And speaking of friends, Jon seemed pretty cool. And he's a boy. Okay. No teasing! He's just nice, that's all. And fun. And he has lovely eyes… Okay, I'll shut up now!

By the time we got back to the house, things were happening quickly. I won't go into the stage-by-stage building of the addition, but before long the log walls were chest high. Then the floor was put down. And the walls got higher. Troy and Lane made some big triangles with boards, and then it was lunchtime.

Lunch was everything I imagined, and more. Our visitors carried our table outside and loaded it with massive amounts of food. They'd even brought plates. Mom donated some food too, and then we all dug in. Kestrel, Jon, and I carried our food out to the horse pasture.

"Is your horse the black one?" I asked Jon.

He nodded, his mouth full of potato salad, then swallowed. "His name is Coal. I got him from the Xeni First Nation last year."

"So he might be a mustang?" asked Kestrel.

Jon nodded.

"Like Twilight." I pointed her out.

"She's a mustang?" asked Jon, focusing on my little buckskin.

"Yeah, she came to live with me this spring."

"Cool. How'd you catch her?"

"It's a long story," I said. "We didn't really catch her. It was more like saving her from a starving wolf. And we both did it, Kestrel and I."

Jon seemed really interested, so we started to tell the whole story, but just as I really got into it, Loonie barked her intruder bark. I looked back toward the cabin to see Charlie riding Redwing into the yard. "I'll tell you the rest later," I promised. "I have to ask Charlie if they caught the poachers."

"Poachers?" Jon asked, his eyes looking as blue as the sky.

"That's why Tumpoo's orphaned," Kestrel explained.

"Yeah," I said, standing up with my plate. "And the poachers caught Charlie and tied him up."

"How'd he get away?"

"I had to save him."

Jon looked at me with raised eyebrows. "*You* saved *Charlie*?"

"Ask him if you don't believe me."

"I didn't say I didn't believe you," he said quickly, jumping up.

The three of us walked back to the group. By the time we got there, Mom had insisted that Charlie eat something and he was filling up his plate with food. I sidled up beside him and took another piece of chicken.

"So did the police catch them?"

He looked at me, a twinkle in his eye. "Who?"

"You know who."

He laughed. I couldn't believe it. Charlie actually laughed.

"So I hear you had some trouble yesterday, Charlie," Troy called from where he sat beside the addition. "Good thing Evy was there to save you."

Charlie grinned sheepishly. "Girls are pretty tough these days."

"Tougher than the old guys, anyway," teased Troy.

Charlie just laughed, and heaped his plate with ham

and coleslaw and scalloped potatoes. When he made his way to one of the logs and sat down, Kestrel, Jon, and I followed.

"So they caught them?" I asked again.

"Yep," he said between bites. "I'm taking the authorities to their campsite tomorrow morning, just in case they were stupid enough to leave any evidence behind. Thought I'd stop by for a bit though and lend a hand. Looks like you two need an addition. It's a pretty small cabin."

"You should try living in it all winter, especially with a crazy artist," I said, only half joking.

After lunch everyone went back to work. Kestrel took the five little kids and fed Tumpoo – I mean, Thumper – again, and Jon and I joined the work crew. Windows were put into log walls and Lane used his chainsaw to cut a door into the main cabin. Large triangles were put up on top of the walls and became the structure for the roof. Plywood went on top of them and then there was a lot of hammering as the shingles were put on.

By the time the structure was finished it was evening. Everyone looked tired, but happy and satisfied. And me? I was exhausted as we sat down to eat the leftovers from lunch. I couldn't believe how much bigger our cabin looked from the outside with the addition. And it had all been done in one day.

An almost overwhelming happiness warmed me as I leaned back and stared at our home illuminated in the evening's soft light and the lanterns scattered about. The first star appeared in the sky directly overtop our house like a promise. I smiled when I thought of the paintings Mom would dream up inside her new studio. She totally deserved this wonderful gift.

When the meal was done people left in groups. First Troy and Lane saddled their horses, and shortly afterward the Robinsons packed all their belongings and headed out, the two-year-old already asleep, snug in the saddle in front of her dad.

I think Mom was especially sad when Caroline and Jon drove off, and I was glad to see it. Caroline had invited us to drop by their place anytime, and I hoped Mom would want to do it now that she'd met her. We waved as they drove out of sight, even though it was probably too dark for them to see us.

Mom sighed when the truck lights disappeared.

"I'll go take care of the horses now," I said, feeling down about the amazing day being almost over. The horses always made me feel better and I really wanted a lift before I said goodbye to Charlie, Kestrel, and her parents.

"There's one more thing to do first. Come inside for a minute, okay?" asked Mom.

"Okay."

Charlie and Seth, Kestrel's dad, were laden down with a heavy looking bundle. I followed them into the studio and watched Seth open the plastic and cut the ties with his knife. The bundle unrolled into the most beautiful rug I'd ever seen – soft blues and greens with touches of purple and vermilion and rose. It looked like the ocean, or how I imagined the ocean would look if I ever saw it. I wanted to lie down and sink into its beauty, it looked so perfect.

"Excuse us," said Mom behind me, and she walked into the room carrying one end of my bed. The other end followed with Elaine and Kestrel lifting it. It hit me like a bolt of lightening. This wasn't going to be a studio. This room was built for another reason. My throat grew tight and tears stung my eyes.

"Where do you want it?" Mom asked me.

I couldn't say anything. I just couldn't.

"Put it over there," said Kestrel, pointing to the window that overlooked the meadow, which is exactly where I would've said if I could've spoken.

They positioned the bed, then Mom, Seth, Elaine, and Charlie left the room, leaving me with Kestrel.

"Is this the coolest surprise or what?"

I nodded, still mute, and then they were all back, Seth and Charlie carrying my worn out, old dresser, Elaine with my chair, and Mom with a big box.

"Here, sit down before you fall down, Evy," said Elaine and positioned the chair behind me.

"And open your early birthday present," added Kestrel.

Mom set the box down in front of me, and for the first time in as long as I could remember my birthday present was a mystery. I still hadn't had a chance to peek.

"I… I… You planned all this?"

Mom laughed, and everyone else smiled. "No, I had a plan for your birthday, but I never would have had your room done in time. Now thanks to our friends, you'll have two celebrations, one with your presents and party, and the other with your cake."

"Open it," Kestrel said impatiently. "I'm dying to see what it is."

The box flaps on top were simply folded, so I pulled it open – to see blues and greens like the rug. And white. White horses in the waves. Rearing and plunging with joy. I lifted it out to discover it was a big, fluffy comforter. Hugging it, I finally found my voice, but babbled so excitedly that I don't know if anything I said made any sense. My mom's eyes shone as if she knew what my gibberish meant.

It was perfect. *Everything* was perfect.

After the big surprise it didn't take long for almost everyone to leave, everyone except Kestrel, who was allowed to stay over again and Charlie, who lingered a bit, chatting with Mom. When Kestrel and I headed out to the barn to give the horses their oats and feed Tumpoo – I mean Thumper – Charlie said he should get going too, and followed us outside. We said goodbye to him as he climbed into Redwing's saddle, and hurried toward the barn. But a few yards shy of the building, I knew I had one more thing to do.

"I'll be back in a sec," I said to Kestrel, and ran

toward the road leading away from our cabin. Charlie had already disappeared.

"Charlie, wait!" I yelled as soon as I rounded the corner.

The hoofbeats stopped. "Yeah?" I heard him turn around in the darkness and walk back toward me. The bulk of the magnificent horse loomed up in front of me. I reached out and stroked his shoulder. He even felt stunning.

"Can I trust you? Really?"

"Always."

"Redwing."

"It's a good name," said Charlie, knowing immediately what I was saying. "Thanks. I'll see you around." Then he turned his horse and rode away.

I walked back to our yard. Kestrel was already heating Tumpoo's milk on the stove and she smiled at me when I entered the barn, then set about feeding the calf. I told Rusty and Twilight about the day's excitement as I prepared their evening meals, refilled water buckets, and gave them a quick grooming.

Twilight interrupted at one point. *What is birthday? The day I was born.*

She snorted and shook her head. *No sense. You not born today.*

I almost laughed out loud.

Humans make no sense sometimes, Rusty explained patiently.

148

I was shocked! If Rusty thought I made no sense, why didn't he ask questions, like Twilight? He rarely disagreed with me and hardly ever questioned.

I reached out and tried to touch his mind, tried to understand – and suddenly, I realized something important. All the times that Rusty never questioned me, I'd assumed he agreed with me. But he didn't keep silent because he agreed or even understood everything I said. He just realized that a lot of things really weren't that important, certainly not important enough to worry about. It was the core stuff that was important, like that I was a good person and someone he could trust, like that I loved him.

You are right, I said, feeling ridiculously complimented. *We humans are silly sometimes.* I mean, compared to horse wisdom, what more could I say?

Before leaving the stall to help Kestrel with Tumpoo, I gave each horse a goodnight hug. As I pulled away from Twilight, I sent one more thought her way, *I like when you ask questions.* And I did, because a new thought had occurred to me. Maybe Twilight wasn't so much mischievous and rebellious as she was curious.

Had I been wrong about her and her independent streak? No. But maybe *some* of what I thought was rebellion was really just her trying to understand. Just like I was trying to understand and was constantly questioning my mom. Questions weren't bad. They didn't mean I was trying to be disrespectful or doubting. They didn't mean I didn't love the one I was questioning. It simply meant that I wanted to understand my world and my place in it, just like Twilight. Someday, like my intrepid filly, I'd get my answers.

When?

I guess time would tell.